DIRTY INTENTIONS

AUBREY BONDURANT

Camie,

The best type
of intentions are
the dirty kind!

♡ Aubrey
Bondurant

ISBN: 978-1726784368
Cover by: Rebecca @The Final Wrap
Text copyright © 2017 by Aubrey Bondurant

Chapter One
DANIELLA

I took a deep breath and smoothed down my wig, thinking the bright pink hair actually made my blue eyes stand out more than did my natural auburn locks. The shimmering silver, barely-covering-my-ass dress and my thigh-high, black suede boots completed the look. Although not quite. Because I was feeling festive and maybe because I needed some metaphoric balls tonight, I put on a pair of ornament earrings.

After all, I was heading to a Christmas party, one being held three days before the holiday. And I wanted to look my absolute best when busting my fiancé for cheating on me.

Yeah, nothing said Merry Christmas quite like sticking your dick in some other chick right before coming home to your loving fiancée for the holidays.

Stuck in the city working on an unfortunate project until tomorrow morning, my ass.

God, how many times over the last year had I fallen for Eric's lines about working late? Too many.

Though we shared a rented townhouse in New Jersey, I'd always been supportive of him keeping an apartment in Manhattan. I'd felt terrible about him having to schlep all the way home after a late night at work. But now I knew better. Too bad I'd already wasted two years with him, but I was determined not to squander one more day.

Of course, I could've waited to confront him at home, but I knew he'd deny it. I'd also lose the advantage of having evidence. So I was going to a party tonight that I knew he'd be attending in order to gather the undeniable proof.

Club Travesty didn't boast a flashy entrance. Matter of fact, it was damn tough to find. I imagined it would be even harder to gain entry into tonight's Christmas party. Which is why I'd cloned Eric's membership card. I'd found it in his inside jacket pocket late one evening when he'd forgotten to take it out. That had been his second misstep. The first was leaving a brochure in his glove compartment which had started my suspicions about this club he belonged to. Then, of course, he'd clearly underestimated me. He had no clue I'd be able to access his online credit card account, discover where the card had been used, and utilize parking stubs to figure out the address of the place. At which point, I'd hacked into his email to see the invitation.

Now that I was taking the fake membership card out of my purse, I fought the nerves. I was good with a computer and details—hell, I'd managed fake ID's in college for me and all my friends—but there was always a chance I'd be caught at the door. Guess Plan B would have to consist of Eric coming home to find I'd moved out all of my things earlier today.

Smiling at the large man in the black suit with the closely cropped hair at the door, I handed him my card. I watched him scan it while trying to steady my heartbeat. The idea of catching Eric in the act made me anxious. But even more did I worry about entering a sex club holiday party for God only knows what. I wondered if I'd thought this through. I mean what if everyone attending was part of an orgy? Or all of a sudden, I became a submissive for a man in a mask with a whip while "Rudolph the Red-Nosed Reindeer" blasted in the background?

Considering how boring my sex life with Eric had been, I'd be lying if I said either thought didn't turn me on a little. Matter of fact, disguised as I was and about to be very single, I found myself eager to see what was inside the club.

Coming out of my weird, holiday-themed, sex-deprived thoughts, I saw the green light flash and smiled at the bouncer who'd allowed me entry. Whew. I'd made it in. But now what?

Now to look like I belonged here. I wasn't sure what I'd expected, but classy chandeliers, posh carpets, and a beautiful Christmas tree front and center hadn't been it. I stepped past the entrance and deeper inside by way of a short hallway. I found myself in the middle of a party. Waitresses in barely-there tuxedo one-piece rompers served champagne while soft holiday music played in the background. So much for a raunchy sex dungeon. I adjusted my mask. My simple black one was nothing compared to some of the more ornate masks I could see around the room.

For a moment, I started to think I might have been mistaken about what type of party this was. Then I noticed the people congregating near the glass on the far side of the room.

Stepping closer to the window, I sucked in a breath. Rooms with glass from floor to ceiling had people on display in various sex acts. The one in front of me boasted two gorgeous women, one of whom was on her back while the other devoured her between her thighs.

Walking down a few feet, I saw the next room featured two men and one woman. She had one cock in her mouth and the other pumping deep inside of her from behind, fast and furious. I was fascinated and hard-pressed to move on from the threesome. But I had to remember I was here for a purpose and tore my eyes away to step down to the next room. I wasn't a prude by any stretch, despite the boring sex I'd been having with my fiancé, but the next scene shocked my senses. In this room a man plowed into a woman missionary-style while another man went to town, thrusting into the first man's ass.

I was about to move on when my gaze locked on the eyes of the man in the middle. The mask made it hard to determine for sure, but the unmistakable birth mark on his left pec absolutely identified him. Holy shit. Eric was not only cheating on me, but he was also bisexual?

I slid out my flash-drive-sized camera and tried to get the right angle. I wanted to get Eric's masked face along with the unmistakable birth mark: tangible evidence. I'd need it since there wasn't exactly a way I could confront him at the moment. Not unless I wanted to bang against the glass and whip off my mask. Although tempting, I would rather show him the proof with the photo. This ought to get his cooperation in returning the money he owed me, my true priority.

I'd given him seventy-five thousand dollars out of my savings to go towards a down payment on the house we planned to buy together. Hindsight made me feel stupid for having trusted him, but when you think you'll spend the rest of your life with someone, what was transferring your savings for your dream home? Unfortunately, my sleuthing revealed he'd spent the money instead of putting it in his nonexistent savings. Evidently, he was a cheater all the way around.

Tucking the camera in my purse and giving one last glance toward Eric, I was about to turn and make my way out when a hand clamped on my elbow and a low voice came in my ear.

"Miss, please follow me."

The man's grip wasn't leaving me much of a choice. A tank in a suit, he was careful, however, make it look as though he was merely guiding me through the crowd. But

4

when he led me into a cleverly hidden elevator near the bar, I had a moment of panic.

"Where are you taking me?"

"To see the boss, ma'am."

"Um, why is that?"

"Don't know, but I reckon you'll find out soon enough."

His Southern voice might be soothing, but his words weren't. Crap. Had they figured out my ID was fake? Or had they spotted the camera? Either way, I was pretty sure I was fucked. And not in a good, sex-club kind of way.

Chapter Two

SHANE

*F*inances didn't wait, not even for Christmas week. This was why, instead of enjoying the party downstairs, I was up in my office crunching numbers, frustrated with our part-time accountant's work or lack thereof. The IRS year-end deadline was looming, but instead of making my profit-and-loss statement his priority tonight, he was downstairs partaking in the festivities. Which is probably what I should have been doing. But ironically, as one of the owners of Club Travesty, I had very little time to indulge in the club's activities.

"Hey, Boss, you coming down?" Heather, my bar manager and long-time loyal employee, came up the stairs. The open loft-like space held both my desk and my best friend's, in addition to a round table and chairs I used for meetings.

I held my head, wanting the break but not in the mood for celebration. Looking up, I tried not to let the stress show. "Not yet. Everything going all right?"

She nodded. "Yep. Good crowd tonight. Sex rooms are hot. Matter of fact, I might be up for something later if, uh, you are."

I forced myself to scan Heather, with her bustier lifting her fake boobs and cinching her tiny waist, and tight leather pants encasing her toned legs. Her hair was long and blond, both of which weren't natural, but it did make her look younger than her thirty-eight birthdays. We'd done acts together over the years, but it had been a while. Mainly because I'd been worried she'd started to catch feelings after the last time. I didn't do feelings with sex.

Regardless, my cock should have stirred. It didn't. I blamed the numbers in front of me. "Maybe some other time, honey." The last thing I wanted to do was hurt her feelings.

"Always happy to take a raincheck. Don't work too hard now."

Right. I'd owned the club with my best friend, Max, for nearly ten years, and I did remember when it used to be fun. Of course what two red-blooded males wouldn't love the idea of running a sex club? But lately it was literally all work and no play. Rubbing my eyes and knowing I still had a long night ahead of me, I stood up from my desk and went through the secure door on my right. There my security team monitored the rooms and the guests on the dozen screens in front of them.

"How's it going, Ron?" I addressed the head of security and the best man I had on the job.

"Nothing out of the ordinary, Mr. Nelson." His scrutinizing gaze never left the screens, scanning for any type of breach in either the sex rooms or the party crowd. Anonymity was the most important thing at Club Travesty, something I took very seriously and the reason I had top security.

"Is Max on the bar?"

"Yes, sir. Any chance he gets."

Not only was Max my best friend from childhood, but he was also my business partner. Whereas I preferred the back office, he enjoyed being in the mix, dealing with personnel and schmoozing. He was the people person. I was not.

Typically, we had a much smaller crowd. But during the

holidays, we did two big VIP parties, one to celebrate Christmas and another on New Year's Eve. This was in addition to the many other services we offered. Private sex rooms for couples who wanted to come in and spice things up, kinky BDSM rooms in the basement, and a newer service I'd added a few years ago which focused on the woman. This included everything from sexual confidence counselors to the "boyfriend experience," where lonely women could come in to gain mojo.

I was just about to step out and back to the books when Ron honed in on something.

"Focus in on camera four," he instructed Alan, his junior security guy.

I wasn't sure what he was looking at until I spotted her. Pink hair that was obviously fake, tight petite body in a silver, curve-hugging dress, and thigh-high boots that were sexy as hell. "What's she holding?"

"Shit. I think it's a camera." He spoke into the intercom, reaching every security guard via their inconspicuous earpieces. "I've got a possible breach. Pink hair, silver dress, black boots. In front of room number four."

Photos were a definite violation of club policy. "Run her credentials," I instructed.

"Yes, sir. You want us to confiscate the device and escort her out?"

That would be the easiest thing to do. But I wanted answers first. "No, bring her up here. Proceed discreetly."

Chapter Three

DANIELLA

he elevator doors opened to a large floor space. Two desks sat in the middle of the room and a bay of one-way mirrors appeared to look down over the main floor. My anxiety was already high, but then I saw him. It went up a whole other level.

Dressed all in black in a well-tailored suit, he walked towards me with a masculine confidence which left no doubt he was in charge. He was gorgeous in a dangerous way with chiseled features, midnight black hair and a scruff that made me wonder what it would feel like between my thighs. Jesus, where had that thought come from? I blamed the sex God in front of me along with the visual from the rooms still on my mind.

He stopped a foot in front me and held out his hand. "May I see your ID card?"

Damn. His husky voice was as sexy as he was.

I swallowed hard before fishing it from my clutch and handing it over. My voice escaped me, though I didn't know whether it was from his presence or from my nerves over the fake ID.

"Scan this." He held it out for Tank Man.

"Yes, sir."

After taking the card, Tank Man opened a door off to the side, offering me a glimpse of monitors.

The moment the door closed, I felt very aware we were alone. The floor may have been spacious, but at that moment it felt anything but. "What, uh, what is this about?" I'd finally found my voice.

"It's about the camera, and the pictures you were taking."

He didn't seem like a man who would appreciate a false runaround, so I didn't bother to deny it. "I'm guessing it's against club rules?"

"You'd guess right. And if you turn it over, I won't press charges."

"You won't press charges against me for taking pictures in a sex club?" As if he would call the cops here. I might be shaking in my boots, but I wasn't stupid.

His smile didn't reach his eyes. "Take off your mask, please."

I swallowed hard but removed it as instructed. Perhaps if I cooperated, he'd be more willing to let me keep the photos.

"I've never seen you here before. What's your name?"

I looked beyond him to where the big man who'd taken my ID was coming out of the door. "I'm sure your human tank can tell you."

His lips twitched, but he simply turned towards his man with a quirked brow.

"Beth Jones, sir. But the membership code belongs to Eric Patterson."

Note to self. When lying and going undercover, wear shoes I could actually run in. These four-inch boots were definitely not fitting the bill if I wanted to make a break for it.

"Go back to your station downstairs, Chad. Send up Lance, please."

"He so didn't look like a Chad," I commented once the

door was closed. Hey, even if I was screwed, I could still be sarcastic.

SHANE

I was the type of man accustomed to having people nervous upon meeting me. I might not be big like the "Tank" she'd referred to, but at six foot one, two hundred pounds, I'd been known to intimidate the people I wanted to. But this woman was cracking jokes. She was challenging me about the police, despite her hands shaking when she'd handed over the ID card and taken off her mask. I appreciated that she hadn't bothered to lie or play dumb.

"Who is Eric Patterson to you?" I hadn't missed the way she'd involuntarily flinched when his name had been mentioned.

She lifted her chin. "My soon-to-be-former fiancé."

"I'm guessing he doesn't know you're here?"

"You'd guess correctly."

She had spunk; I'd give her that. "What are the pictures for?"

"Well, nothing says insurance better than a photo of your former fiancé fucking another woman while getting it in the ass at the same time by a dude."

If this wasn't so serious, then I might have grinned at her choice of words. "Insurance against what? You're a woman who came in tonight to get proof your fiancé was cheating. So now go home, throw his clothes out, and do whatever you women do to get your revenge, but leave my club out of it."

She gritted her teeth. "I have something that could be useful to you."

I raised a brow, slowly scanning up from her fuck-me, thigh-high boots to the short dress that gave me a glimpse of skin. Her breasts, although not large, were certainly real. And despite the fact she was wearing a lot of makeup, I could see that under it she was beautiful. For a moment, I wanted nothing better than to rip off her wig to see the color of her hair. But the murderous glare she was shooting me gave me pause, not to mention amusement.

"Jesus. Are all men pigs? I meant your damn security system. Obviously, I'm not throwing myself at the owner of a sex club. I'm not that pathetic."

Normally I didn't give a shit what people thought about me, having perfected such an art form years ago. But this particular woman's audacity to think herself too good for me snapped my temper. "I can assure you I'd rather jerk off than fuck someone vanilla like you."

I immediately saw the hurt flash in her eyes and instantly regretted my words. I'd made this personal when it was only business.

"I'm sure my fiancé had the same thought. And the insurance I speak of is because he took my money, and I want it back." She dug in her clutch and handed over a small camera. "I'll be going now unless you have any other insults you'd prefer to hurl before I do."

Unbelievable. "As if implying you'd never stoop so low as to sleep with me wasn't starting it."

Her pretty face showed confusion. "What the hell are you talking about? You know what? It doesn't matter. I need to go."

I was about to let her. Getting the camera should have been enough, but I needed to address one more thing. How had she gotten in tonight?

My gaze landed on Lance coming out of the elevator. He'd been on the door when Ms. Beth Jones—which couldn't be her real name—had come through.

"Wait one moment. Lance, do you remember letting this woman in the door earlier tonight?"

Lance assessed her quickly but shook his head. "Sorry, sir.

I don't remember her. There were a lot of women dressed similarly tonight."

"Yes, but this one gave you a fake ID. It might have looked authentic, but it was cloned from the card of a male member, which she is definitely not. That you should've caught. Clear out your things. You're fired."

She gasped. "What? No. You can't fire him."

DANIELLA

The arrogant asshole had the nerve to arch a brow at me.

"I'm the owner. I can do whatever I like."

"Yes, sir. Sorry, sir." Lance spoke up, ready to leave.

Could I help it if my guilt was heavy? I'd come to expose a cheater, not make some poor guy lose his job. "No, wait. I'll show you how I cloned the cards. That's what I was offering before. But if I show you, then you have to let, uh, Lance keep his job. You have a serious security breach with the way your cards are designed."

I watched him contemplate. "Are you a computer hacker?"

"No, just really good with them."

"And how are you with accounting? Because if I dismiss Eric from the club, I'm going to be without an accountant."

My eyes widened. "You let Eric handle your books? Are you a client of his firm?"

"No. He did this on the side to compensate for his, uh, membership fee. He is an accountant, is he not?"

"Yeah, one who stole money and doesn't have the accu-mulated wealth he boasts about." I used air quotes to high-light the last few words.

Although his face said nothing, the set of his jaw told me everything. "Lance, go downstairs and bring Mr. Patterson up here. I have some questions for him."

"Does that mean Lance isn't fired?"

"It would seem so. For now."

Tank Two simply nodded. "Yes, sir. I'll bring Mr. Patterson up."

"How did you find out he was stealing?"

"I gave him seventy-five thousand dollars to go with his supposed two hundred thousand for a down payment on a house. None of it is in his bank accounts. Matter of fact, the statements show he's exclusively been withdrawing money for months."

"Excuse me?"

"When I hacked into his bank accounts, none of my money was there. But I did see it used to be, along with a couple hundred thousand, but it's all been withdrawn. That's why I need the pictures from tonight, as insurance he'll give my money back."

"I take it he wouldn't want people finding out he was in a threesome with another man?"

"He'd freak out if I let the pictures go to all of his buddies or coworkers."

"Are you sure you want to see him? I could just as easily do this without you here. The last thing I want is for you to start crying or get hysterical."

Seriously? "The answer to your insulting question would be no, I won't start freaking out."

Matter of fact, I was more than ready to confront Eric.

Chapter Four

SHANE

I watched Eric come off the elevator doors. He took off the mask and gave me a smile before his gaze flicked over to my guest.

"Daniella. That's not you, is it?"

She ripped the pink wig off her head, letting auburn locks flow down her back and making it clear she was the person he'd guessed.

She was even prettier without the wig, with her natural dark red hair cascading down her back in waves, but it was the fire in her eyes which made her stunning. Although I'd hauled him up here wanting answers about his alleged stealing—he was acting as my accountant, after all—like a sick voyeur, I was riveted to the spot. I wanted to find out what would happen once she confronted him over the cheating.

"What the hell are you doing here?" Eric asked, still clearly in shock.

"Shouldn't that be my question for you?"

She was calm. I'd give her that.

"I, uh, I mean some people from the office—we were working late and—"

"Oh, my God. Even now you lie. After I saw you getting fucked in the ass by some guy ten minutes ago."

Eric went pale at her remark, and I have to say it made me happy. I'd never really liked the guy on a personal level and wasn't surprised to find he was a cheater. The question was whether he was a thief. If he was, I was going to break his face.

"What do you expect? You're boring as hell in the bedroom. No boobs, no adventure—"

"No cock," she supplied, arching a brow.

At least she wasn't about to let him insult her. There was no way it couldn't have stung, though, especially after my earlier comment.

"As enlightening as it would be to hear you two go back and forth all night, I don't have the time. But I do have a vested interest in bringing you up here, Eric."

His gaze shifted to me, and I could see it. The nervousness. "Uh, what's that?"

"Are you stealing from me?"

"No. No way, Shane."

I raised a brow at his familiarity.

"I mean Mr. Nelson, sir."

"Did you steal from her?"

His eyes got big, and he turned red. "No. She's my fiancée."

"Not any more I'm not."

She took off the ring and tossed it onto a nearby table. If she'd been smart, she would've used it for leverage to ensure he returned her money first, but I stayed quiet. And in fact, before he could step over to grab the considerably sized diamond ring, she snatched it up.

"Return my money, and you can have it back."

"What? That ring is worth over ten grand. All precedents says the man gets the ring back if an engagement is broken."

Dumbass. But then again, this was the most amusement I'd had in weeks.

"I'm aware of what legal precedents says. However, if the man owes her seventy-five thousand dollars, the ring can be held as collateral. I want it all returned."

"It was to go towards a house, so good luck proving anything."

I'd had enough of this asshole. It bothered me that he wasn't apologizing or appeared to show any remorse. She'd trusted him, and he'd betrayed her trust: not only by cheating, but also by taking her money. Neither of which was sitting well with me. "What do you think the guys at the office or your buddies would think of your little threesome downstairs tonight, Eric?"

His face started to turn a deep red. Although he was a handsome guy, if you preferred the Wall Street type, he certainly didn't look it now. Matter of fact, he looked like he was about to puke. Which meant I had his number.

"You can't threaten me with that. Anonymity is rule one with the club."

I shrugged. "I can't, but she can. She has pictures."

His eyes darted back and forth between us. "But that's against club rules."

"Well, see, that's a predicament. She's not actually a club member. In fact, you're in violation for allowing her to use your card tonight to get in."

"I didn't. She must've copied it."

"Which means she had access to it, which ultimately constitutes carelessness on your part."

"What do you want from me?"

"The truth. Are you stealing from me?"

"No. Definitely not."

Considering he didn't have access to my actual bank accounts but only to the reports, I chose to believe him. "Fine, but if I find one penny gone, those pictures go viral at your firm. Also, you'll return all the money to Ms.—"

"Trivioli," she supplied.

Daniella Trivioli. The name rolled around in my mind.

"Okay. Fine," he readily agreed.

"And do not come back here. Your membership has been revoked."

Now he looked like he was on the verge of crying. He certainly hadn't been as upset to lose his supposed future life partner. "Please, don't do that."

"I don't tolerate thieves or liars, Eric. Now, I suggest you leave without a scene before I make one and have you tossed out."

He turned, but not without walking in front of Daniella and mumbling something which made her go completely pale.

"What did you just say to her?"

"Nothing." Eric appeared in a hurry to be going.

I moved closer to step in front of her. "What did he say to you?" I might be a dick, but the last thing I'd allow was the victim in this situation to be made to feel worse. This woman, in particular, was pulling out a protective side I hadn't felt in years.

"He said 'have a nice life, you frigid orgasmless cunt.'"

I raised a brow. "He's never given you an orgasm?" Why the fuck did women stay with men who couldn't get them off? Monogamy was a foreign concept to me, especially if, at the very least, the sex wasn't good.

She swallowed hard. Tears glistened in her prideful gaze. "Not often."

Eric scoffed. "Because you take too long."

There was a reason my club offered sexual confidence classes. Because men like Eric systematically shredded a woman's self-assurance by being selfish in bed. I stepped closer to Daniella. My arm went around her waist, pulling her to my side. I'd be lying if I said her warmth didn't affect me. Her soft curves could be felt under the flimsy excuse for a dress she was wearing.

"I find it funny you'd automatically assume the problem is her." I let my hand wander down her side slowly, seductively, while I told myself I was helping her save face. "Because your ex-fiancée is a beautiful, sexy woman." I stepped behind her then, my one hand still splayed on her hip, the other inching up her skirt in the back.

How far would she be willing to let this go? Any moment I expected her to step away. At the same time, I hoped she wouldn't.

"But she's clearly been sexually deprived for a long time. But don't worry, Eric. She's come to the right place to remedy that." Before I could think about the ramifications or the fact that Daniella wasn't the typical guest at Club Travesty, my hand went up her skirt and between her legs.

DANIELLA

I was absolutely frozen—no pun intended with the frigid comment. I could feel Shane's breath on the back of my neck, his hand burning into my skin despite the layer of dress material between them, and now his other hand creeping up the back of my skirt. And I was doing absolutely nothing to stop it.

"As far as her cunt is concerned..."

Oh, God. His finger lightly ghosted between my legs at the wet silk thong. I found myself closing my eyes and gripping his arm, wanting—no, needing—more.

"It's hot and wet."

His whisper, meant only for my ears, caused goosebumps. "Tell me if you want me to stop now. Otherwise, I'm going to put my fingers inside you and make you come."

Even if I could've formed the words, there was no way I was speaking at the moment. In addition to being wildly turned on by the man since the moment I'd laid eyes on him, curiosity had me wondering if, in fact, the problem all along hadn't been me. I'd beaten myself up plenty for not being able to have a proper orgasm. So, with the hot guy offering, why the hell not? And although this was very un-Daniella of me, I suddenly felt uninhibited about having this sexy stranger behind me, giving me the pleasure I'd never experienced with the man who supposedly loved me.

My eyes flew open the moment he inserted a finger. Despite being a complete stranger, he was unapologetic with his tutorial in front of our audience of Eric and the bouncer. I might be covered by my dress in front, but I don't think it would've mattered if I hadn't been. Because I was lost in sensation. A breath left me when he wasted no time in inserting two and then curled them up deep inside of me where he started to move them against a spot that made my knees weak.

"You see, Eric, I could've gone for the easy target of her clit. Given her a nice climax by rubbing her there. But I think after the lack of orgasms she's received from you for—how long was it?"

Jesus, was he actually asking me a question?

"Two years," I offered on a whisper, digging my nails into his arm around my waist. I hoped he was fully prepared to take the majority of my weight as I could feel my legs start to shake.

"After two years, she deserves a G-spot orgasm which will rip through her body and have her coming like a porn star."

He wasn't too far off. The moment he started pressing his two fingers up against a spot I hadn't known existed, a moan escaped my throat.

"Get out," Shane grunted.

I flicked my gaze towards Eric's face just in time to see it heat with humiliation before he was escorted out. I didn't care because my climax slammed into me with full force, taking both my breath and my ability to remember it was a stranger's fingers doing this to me.

"That's it. Ride it out."

His breath came in my ear, the huskiness of his voice causing an involuntary shiver. My body bucked against his hand, leaving me completely spent in the aftermath. Calming my breath, both hands gripping his forearm, I heard myself whimper when he withdrew his fingers.

"Are you okay to stand?"

I nodded, still unable to form words. Fortunately, the desk was next to me so I could use my hand to brace my legs, which remained shaking.

"So, I guess, thanks for that." What else do you say when a stranger finger-fucks you to the best orgasm of your life?

He chuckled. "You're welcome. Now, what?"

My gaze met his, and I felt my face heat. Something about meeting the man in the eyes after he'd had his fingers inside of me was disconcerting. Gone was the wild girl who'd wanted to be someone else tonight, and back was the reality of the jilted fiancée who'd come here for proof. This whole night was past the point of surreal. "Um, I should leave."

He frowned. "Where will you go?"

"I have my stuff in my car and need to get a hotel room."

"It's three days before Christmas, so that's not happening in Manhattan."

I hadn't thought much past busting Eric. Now that the adrenaline was fading, thanks in part to the whole orgasm thing, I was bone weary, in need of a warm shower and a comfortable bed. "I guess I'll head back towards Jersey, then. I don't know."

"I thought you were going to show me how you cloned the ID."

"Now?"

"You want Lance to keep his job, right?"

My temper suddenly flared at his use of power. But I wasn't angry enough to take a chance on him firing the unfortunate guy who'd let me in tonight. "Fine. Get your computer guy in here, and give me an hour. But that's it. If he can't keep up, it's not my problem."

He grinned. "My computer guy is out until the day after Christmas. So how about you show me instead? And rest assured I'll have no problem keeping up."

I swallowed hard at the innuendo. For some reason, I couldn't bring myself to tell him I was too tired or too emotionally exhausted. He was challenging me, and I couldn't back down. Fine. Game on, Mr. Magic Fingers.

Chapter Five

SHANE

*S*he was smart. And running on empty by the look of her. But pride had been pushing her through the last twenty minutes as she walked me through her cloning process. Part of me felt guilty, but the other part knew that once she left here, I'd never see her again. I reasoned that I pushed her into staying because I needed to figure out how she'd cloned the card.

Truth was, I wouldn't have fired Lance for more than the five minutes it would've taken to make my point. He'd made a mistake, and I was annoyed. More interesting was how she'd reacted to it. Not many people gave a shit about people they didn't know. But she'd been outraged enough to stay and show me the security breach.

I listened raptly while she explained the flaw in our card chipping. Damn if she wasn't right. It was a design flaw. Frankly, a more sophisticated hacker, one who hadn't simply wanted photos of her ex engaging in group sex, could've exploited it a lot worse.

"And that's it. With the updated chip technology, you should be fine."

"But you're not a computer programmer?"

She blushed, probably not liking such a personal question. People got weird about protecting their identity in a place like Club Travesty. "No, but working with computers has always been my hobby."

"Is that what you call hacking these days?"

She smiled. "Gotta learn how to develop before you can hack code. I'm just good at guessing passwords. Most people aren't very smart with what they use."

"Meaning Eric?"

She sighed. "Yeah. His password was his favorite sports team. Your chip is simply outdated technology. No hacking involved, actually."

She stood up, stifling a yawn. It was after midnight, and considering the kind of night she'd had, I imagined she was exhausted.

"I have an extra bed in the back if you want to crash. At this hour, you're not going to find a hotel room."

"Really?" She looked relieved.

I wasn't sure why the hell I was offering her my bed, especially when I'd had every intention of jerking off there to the smell of her on my fingers. Which was stupid considering I had an abundance of pussy to choose from downstairs. Perhaps taking advantage of that was what I needed to do to get this woman out of my head.

She bit her lip, looking uncertain. "I don't want to impose."

"I wouldn't offer if it was an imposition. There's a private bathroom, and nobody will bother you."

"I, um—That would be great. I'll go get my suitcase from my car in the garage."

I shook my head, the protective vein tapped again. "Not dressed like that by yourself. Give me the keys, and I'll have one of the tanks do it."

She smiled, clearly liking my newly adopted nicknames for the two giant bouncers. "I'm not taking your bed, am I?"

"I have plans downstairs, so no." I didn't miss the way disappointment flashed in her expression. But the last thing I needed was her thinking the bed meant anything. In an effort to be clear, I said, "And this is simply a favor for showing me the faulty chip design. By morning, I expect you gone."

Fire shone in her eyes and straightened her spine. "You know, I can resolve that issue right now. Goodbye."

Shit. I'd gone too far. "Wait. Look, you're dead on your feet. And I'm an asshole. Okay?"

She quirked a brow. "Yes, but one of those things will be better by tomorrow. Although I appreciate your half-ass attempt at an apology, the answer is no. Good night, Mr. Nelson, and, uh, take care."

Without a glance back, she walked out.

AFTER CALLING one of my tanks to ensure he followed at a respectable distance to see her safely to her car, I decided to do some research. Then I had to enter the craziness of the party. It was approaching the witching hour for fights, drunks, and anything else that might come up.

I typed her name into a search engine. Holy shit. According to LinkedIn, Daniella Trivioli was a tax attorney. I went to the law firm's website and searched out her bio. No picture, which was disappointing. But the site did tell me she'd attended NYU and was licensed to practice in both New York and New Jersey. Considering the New York bar was nothing to sneeze at, she had to be as smart as I'd sensed.

This could be the answer to my issues with the IRS. Although I could've hired any number of professionals to help me with my accounting problems, I decided to hire myself this particular tax attorney. I told myself it was because fate had brought her here tonight when I had an issue with the IRS. I only hoped she'd believe the lie better than I did.

Chapter Six

DANIELLA

"*A*sshole," I muttered under my breath as I went down the stairs from his office. Unfortunately, I wasn't looking where I was walking and knocked right into a handsome man coming up.

"Whoa, there. Sorry. You okay?" The tall man with light brown hair and an easy smile steadied me.

"Yeah. Sorry. I wasn't watching where I was going. Excuse me." I attempted to move past him, but he stepped in front of me.

"It's okay. So who's the asshole?" His gaze, filled with humor, flicked up the stairs.

"Judging by the look on your face, you already know. Sorry, I really must be leaving."

His grin widened. "You're the one they caught taking pictures, aren't you?"

My face heated. "I, uh—yeah. And I really need to go." I started to feel uncomfortable. This was a sex club, and I had no idea what this guy was thinking by not allowing me to pass.

As if reading my mind, he said, "Relax. I'm one of the

owners. The name is Max. And I take it you met the other half?"

I let out a breath. "Yes. And everything is set now. He has the camera."

"You sure it's set? You look a little pissed."

"Considering Mr. Nelson is your partner, I don't think you're surprised he has that effect on people. Now, then, I have a hotel room to find."

"Won't be easy three days before Christmas."

It irked me that everyone seemed to think of this but me. "So I've heard. Good night, Max."

He stepped aside. "Good night, uh—"

"Daniella." I provided my real name before I could think about it. Oh, well. Wasn't like I was coming back here anyhow.

"Good night, Daniella."

———

WAKING up the next morning in my hotel bed, I tried to tell myself today was just another day. So what if it was Christmas Eve tomorrow and most people were traveling to be with their families? So what if I'd had to drive back over to Jersey City in order to find a room for the night? So what if everything I owned was either in my car or in the small storage unit I'd rented until I could get my money back and find a new place?

It was tempting to call in sick to work today, but with nothing but a pity party in front of me, I decided not to. I might not emphatically enjoy my job—come on, it was taxes; how much fun could that possibly be?—it wasn't like me to shirk my responsibility, either. Especially with my savings gone and the need to get another apartment soon. Although it wasn't busy yet for tax season, most of it picking up after the end of the year, I had a few cleanup tasks which could keep me busy.

Too bad my parents had already left on their Caribbean cruise. I'd had no interest in going with them initially, happy to have the excuse to stay home because Eric was working. But now the thought of spending the holiday alone seemed even worse than spending it with my difficult parents. Of course, if my mother found out about the breakup, I would've been jumping overboard to get away from her disappointment. When she did find out there would be no wedding to plan, she was going to be devastated.

She would be the only one. As I took stock of my feelings after rolling out of bed, I realized I wasn't.

Instead I felt a tremendous relief. So then, why hadn't I ended things sooner? The question stuck with me while I was in the shower and through a big room-service breakfast. Unfortunately, I didn't like the answer. I'd been going through the motions, checking off the boxes in life, instead of being in love with him.

When my cell phone on the desk rang, I shoved the thoughts to the side. It was Eric. And I knew I had to get this over with sooner or later.

"Hello."

"It's about damn time. I've been calling you all night."

I had absolutely no patience for him. "What do you want?"

"Where are you?"

"None of your business."

"Come on, Daniella. This isn't you. Be reasonable. We can work things out."

"Seriously? Because I think after finding out you stole money from me, are bisexual and cheating on me, and then had the audacity to call me a frigid cunt last night, that reconciling is the last thing on my mind."

"I'm sorry. I wasn't myself. And Shane putting his hands on you. What the hell was that about?"

It was reckless, freeing, and completely without regret. "It was about finding one more reason never to see you again. In two minutes he gave me what you've never been able to. Now listen up. You owe me seventy-five thousand dollars. I want it, or I go to the authorities and things get messy."

"That's blackmail."

"No, that's giving you a chance before you lose your job over me filing embezzlement charges. Blackmail would be if I threatened to show those pictures of you taking it up the ass by the blond-haired fellow to everyone we know, including your boss."

My implication held heavy on the line until he finally spoke.

"I— Shit. Okay. I can only get you half right now. But I promise the other half will be coming."

"You have two days to wire half and two weeks to come up with the rest."

"Then will you return the ring? It belonged to my grandmother."

A reminder to get him to sign a receipt of return because he'd probably hock it and then tell his mother I kept it. "Of course. I want to hold onto it about as much as I want to hold onto our relationship. And if I get tested and find out I have something, the gloves are completely off. I hope you realize that."

"I'm clean. I swear. I always used condoms. And since we used condoms, too, we should be good."

"Hope so. Two days, and I want half the money. I'll text you the account information."

"I have it already, don't I?"

I laughed without humor. "As if I wouldn't have changed my bank accounts after learning you stole from me. Goodbye, Eric."

I sat there humming with adrenaline but still no tears. Two years gone with that man, and I was more pissed at being duped than upset at losing him.

Chapter Seven

SHANE

I wasn't a man who enjoyed waiting. So I'd had a conversation with Daniella's boss in the morning and expected her any minute.

"You look smug. You finally give the numbers a rest and get laid?" Perched on the side of my desk, Max thumbed through the mail.

I glanced up from my computer. "I'm not smug. Just waiting."

He cocked a brow. "For what?"

My gaze traveled towards the elevator doors where Chad appeared with my guest. She didn't look too happy to see me.

"What in the hell are you doing calling my firm and requesting me?" Daniella's eyes were fiery while her tone was frosty.

I lifted a brow, allowing myself the pleasure of eye-fucking her from head to toe and enjoying the hell out of the way she was blushing at the scrutiny. She was dressed like an office fantasy. Her petite figure was encased in a long black pencil skirt that accented her hips. A dark blue, collared shirt showed off a tease of skin at the column of her throat. Pearls in both her ears and around her neck set off the professional image. But it was the black stilettos which gave me pause. Made me fantasize about them digging into my back as I pounded into her on my desk.

"I need a tax attorney." It was a shit answer to rile her up even further. I wasn't disappointed.

She huffed. "Then you could've discussed it with me rather than call my boss and demand I be on site this morning."

"You mean last night when you told me that you were a tax attorney?" It still annoyed me she hadn't revealed this.

"Sir, do you need me for anything else?" Chad looked awkward about witnessing our exchange.

"No, thank you. Max, you can go, too."

I couldn't explain it, but I didn't like the way he was looking at her. Suddenly, I wanted us to be alone.

"Are you kidding me? I'm enjoying the hell out of this. And I'm Max, by the way, the more charming of the owners."

Much to my amusement, Daniella didn't so much as give him a glance. "We met last night."

"Holy shit. Daniella from the stairs?"

What the hell? When had he met her, and how did he know her name?

"I must say the dress last night was fantastic, but you look more beautiful now." Max stepped in front of her, extending his hand. Doing what he did best, he kissed it.

But instead of smiling shyly or giggling like most women did when Max was romantic, she merely lifted a brow and retracted her hand.

Max glanced over at me and spoke in perfect Italian. "Wow, she really has eyes only for you, my friend. Although whether they are the kind that want you to fuck her or the kind that want you dead, I'm not sure."

My gaze didn't waver from Daniella's.

She didn't miss a beat, replying in equally perfect Italian.

33

"The latter one definitely. And don't you know it's rude to switch to another language in front of someone?"

Turning uncharacteristically pink, he apologized in English. "I'm sorry. You're right. It was rude. How do you know Italian?"

"My name is Daniella Maria Trivoli." The 'duh' was implied by her very Italian name.

He laughed out loud. "Should've guessed as you've certainly got the temper for it. But the blue eyes and red hair don't exactly announce the fact."

"I was adopted by Italian parents; my DNA says I'm mostly Irish."

"Good thing an Irish temper is only a legend," he chuckled, causing her to smile.

The fact that she was offering up these tidbits of her life him was starting to grind on me. "Max, if there isn't anything else, Ms. Trivoli and I have business."

Laughter came from his chest. "I bet. I'll leave you two. And Daniella, if he's an asshole to you again, you can always find me at the bar."

She waited until he went down the stairs to speak again. "What do you want from me, Shane?"

It was a good thing I was sitting down because hearing her call me by my first name had my cock instantly hard. "I need a good accountant, one especially expert at taxes. The IRS is up our ass, and your boss assures me you're one of the best."

"I'm a tax attorney, not an accountant."

"You have a CPA, do you not?"

"I don't work in Manhattan. I work in New Jersey."

"But you're licensed to work in New York, too. I checked. I'll pay for your accommodation in the hotel next door as soon as they have rooms available. In the meantime, you can take the bedroom here or commute from wherever you're staying. I'll need you for at least the next week. I've made it very lucrative for your firm, assuring your boss I'll pay double time for the short notice."

I knew she was caught between a rock and a hard place.

"It's Christmas Eve tomorrow, so I can come back the day after Christmas to get started."

"This is time sensitive."

She was incredulous. "Meaning you want me to work through the holiday?"

"Did you have other plans?" It was a dick question considering those plans had most likely been with her ex-fiancé. But I wasn't exaggerating when I said it was urgent. If I didn't get my numbers fixed by the first of the year, we could be screwed at tax time.

"Fine. I'll stay here until the hotel opens up. But my things are at a hotel in Jersey City."

"I'll have Chad go fetch them." And bring them to the bedroom where I slept when I didn't make it home, which was a lot these days. The idea of her using my bed made it all the more appealing to fuck her. But I wasn't giving in to the temptation.

Although I might picture pounding into Ms. Daniella Trivoli until she screamed my name, there were three things keeping me from acting.

One, she was rebounding from her douche bag ex-fiancé. Although I was an asshole in my own right, I wasn't the type who tried to be one on purpose or who wanted to deal with the fallout of a rebound.

Two, I desperately needed to get the mess of accounting in front of me fixed before it screwed over this club on account of both taxes and losses.

And lastly, she wasn't the type of girl up for a quick fuck. She had strings written all over her. I'd learned to be crystal clear in my intentions.

"Hand over your key and jot down the hotel name and room number. I'll have everything transferred here."

"Actually, I have an appointment first, but I can come back after."

I narrowed my eyes. She could be trying to find a way to get back to her office and out of the assignment. "What appointment?"

I didn't expect the answer she gave me.

"I need to get tested. Despite Eric insisting he used condoms elsewhere, I don't want to take any chances." Her neck turned red with her admission.

My voice showed my sympathy for her situation. "I have an in-house person who can do that for you here. We insist on the staff getting tested monthly. It would be done discreetly, and you'd have the results by tomorrow."

"Thank you. That would be better than the humiliation of going to my gynecologist hoping they have a walk-in available."

"I'll set it up while you get started here and have her come up when she's ready." I slid a notepad and pen to her.

She wrote down the name of her hotel, the Doubletree in Jersey City, along with the room number. "My car is there, too, as I took the train into the city."

"I'll have it brought over, as well." I watched her now write down the description of the gray Honda Accord. Practical, just like her.

She handed over her keycard and the car keys. "Fine. Thank you."

I stood up, offering her my seat.

She took out a small laptop and notepad before fixing her stunning blue eyes on me. "Of all the tax attorneys and high-powered accountants in the city who could take on a business like yours, why do you want me here?"

Good fucking question. One I'd never admit had something to do with the mysterious effect she had on me.

"I'm not a trusting person, Ms. Trivioli."

She arched a brow. "I clone your membership card, sneak

36

in, take pictures against club policy, and suddenly you trust me?"

"No, but you didn't lie about it once you got caught. Obviously, you have a sense of justice. Otherwise, you wouldn't have wanted to confront your ex. Nor would you have stayed to show me the way you cloned the card to ensure Lance kept his job. I don't tolerate liars."

Her shoulders relaxed, and I was afforded a wry smile. "That'll be a refreshing change. Anything else I should know?"

I leaned in closer towards her. I couldn't help myself. "Yes. I expect loyalty and discretion from my employees. I've already run your background check and will give you a pass for the employee entrance." I handed her the key card from my pocket and watched her take it in her hand.

The scent of a soft musky fragrance made me want to inhale deeply. This close, I could make out the dusting of freckles across the bridge of her nose. She practically shouted innocence. But once again, it was the fire in her eyes which intrigued me.

"First off, I'm not your employee. As far as discretion is concerned, I think we both have enough of a vested interest to ensure that happens. But my loyalty is something earned. So for now, let's agree that I'll work hard for you and keep the club secrets. Deal?"

My lips twitched at her spunk. "Deal."

"Now, let's start with what the problem is."

I laid out the facts. Our numbers weren't adding up. We were experiencing losses even while revenue was increasing. If I didn't have a good reason to report a loss to the IRS, they'd be up my ass.

"I put everything in a spreadsheet on the computer in front of you. I'll get a nondisclosure agreement, then give you whatever else you need for backup."

I watched, fascinated, for the better part of a half hour

while Daniella examined my tax returns from the last five years and my computer ledger. I finally left her to it after a few pointed glares told me to leave her be. Plus, I wanted to give her privacy when Shelly came up to take her blood for the test.

When I came back up for lunch, I was surprised to see Daniella had already obtained the folder of receipts for the past year and dumped them all over my desk.

DANIELLA

Luckily, Shelly was completely professional in taking my blood then minutes after Shane had left me. I wasn't sure what he'd told her, but the woman smiled and told me she'd provide the results tomorrow. I really was grateful to get this out of the way.

About two hours after I'd taken a seat, Chad returned with my things, as promised. Although staying here was unorthodox, it helped me out. With the holidays, it would be nearly impossible to find a new apartment right now. After New Year's, the search would hopefully be easier. And since Eric had wiped out my savings, I was grateful to avoid wasting money on hotel rooms at holiday prices.

After another hour, Shane returned. I could tell in one glance he was none too happy to find me going through all the backup detail. But what did he expect? I was on the clock. Although I didn't know why he'd asked me here, I'd be damned if I wouldn't give this job my best. Which meant being thorough. Plus, if I was being honest, I was intrigued by a business such as this.

But at the moment, I was starving. Judging from the smell of whatever he was carrying, he'd at least brought lunch.

"Great. You brought food. I'm hungry."

"What are you doing? How did you get these?" He strode over, set the paper bag on the desk, and scanned my notes.

"I'm doing what you're paying me for."

"You haven't signed a disclosure yet. You can't look at all of this."

I slid the signed document in front of him. "Here. Max came up and gave it to me when he brought the receipts." Whereas Shane was closed off and hard to read, Max was friendly and helpful.

His gaze didn't leave mine. Irritation reflected in his eyes, most likely because I'd taken control by starting on the books without his permission. Oh, well, time to get the fuck over it.

"I didn't give the green light—"

I held up my hand. "No, you didn't. But looking at a trial balance and tax returns is not enough. I need the details in order to do a proper audit. Anyhow, if you want to eat lunch with me, you can tell me why it is you're losing revenue and could trigger an IRS audit if you report a loss. I'm all ears."

I hadn't set out to piss him off with my words, but the vision of the vein throbbing on the side of his head was pretty hot. So was his barely contained temper. I wasn't typically one to play with fire, but somehow Shane pushed all my buttons, including those I hadn't realized I owned.

"If I knew, I wouldn't have you here. The numbers can't be correct because our membership rates are up."

I lifted a brow, trying to ignore the masculine scent of him. A mixture of mint, body wash, and pure, virile male. "I'll focus on your costs, then. Maybe they've grown. How long has Eric done your books?" Although my ex was not trustworthy, I'd never known him to be a sloppy accountant.

He shook his head. "The last two years. I did them before that."

"Explain how the business works, according to the IRS. I mean, obviously, they don't know you're a sex club."

He sighed but took a seat while digging out the contents

from the bag and handing over a cheesesteak. "Club Travesty is a bar and membership-only club. We operate as such."

"Then how do members pay for sex?"

He shook his head. "Careful, that would be illegal. Members do not pay for sex. They pay for a membership, which allows them certain perks. The sort of perks depend on the level of membership. We have everything from the basic level, which has been very popular over the last few years and is essentially sexual counseling, to what we call our boyfriend package, and on to the hard-core, dominant-submissive type of play."

"What is the boyfriend package?" Rather than wanting to know for tax purposes, I found myself fascinated.

"It's where women can take sexual lessons. Gain back their confidence or learn—"

"To have a proper orgasm?"

Suddenly I realized my interest was much more than just gaining a working knowledge of the club.

*H*er question wasn't glib; it was genuinely curious. It was a good thing I was seated as her simply mentioning an orgasm got me hard. "Yes."

She smiled. "You're like Robin Hood, then. Only instead of gold and coins to the poor and unfortunate, you're giving orgasms."

I threw my head back and laughed. "And I make a profit from it."

She frowned, and I realized I'd inadvertently implied she should've paid for it. I was about to clarify, but she lobbed her next question.

"Mostly women sign up for these services?"

"Yes. But we have other services which are nonsexual."

"Like what?"

"Sexual confidence counseling. We started it at Max's suggestion, and it's been really popular. However, we did have to fire the manager recently."

"For what?"

"Pushing some of the guys who only did counseling into more physical aspects. Unfortunately, we lost a couple good employees. Some women need a place to go to ask questions and discover or regain their mojo. It should be up to the two of them whether to make it physical or not."

"Is that why you did what you did in front of Eric? To help me regain my mojo?"

I swallowed hard, not wanting to analyze my motives or have her do so. "It pisses me off to have any woman told the problem is her. I especially didn't like the way he did it."

Our gazes locked until she finally looked away.

"I'll look to see if losing some employees and their clientele could be some explanation for the loss of revenue." She made a note. "And last night. The Christmas party. Is that a common thing to do?"

I was happy for the change in subject. "It was one of our VIP parties. On a typical night, we allow our VIPs to reserve those rooms for group play activities. These can range from private settings to the more public type that you witnessed."

"People enjoy having sex while others watch?"

A smile curved my lips as I thought about Ms. Proper in front of a crowd. "Absolutely. Others enjoy finding new partners or adding a plus one. You'd be surprised how many couples come in looking for a third party, simply to spice things up."

"Do you partake in these, uh, demonstrations?"

Although her question wasn't meant to be judgmental, I found myself defensive. "Upon occasion, yes."

But it wasn't judgment in her eyes; it was a heavy dose of lust. Interesting. I'd long ago learned the signs of a woman aroused, and Ms. Daniella Trivioli was just that.

"What types of things do you do?"

My gaze laser focused on hers. "The dirty kind. I need to get back downstairs. Let me know if you have any questions on the receipts you're going through."

I abruptly got up. Daniella might not know it, but she was dangerous. She represented everything I didn't want. Strings, rebound, vanilla. Those were only a few of the terms I bounced around in my head as I took the stairs down to the main level. Besides, she was here to do a job, which didn't include fucking me—no matter how her eyes lit up at the possibility of me performing.

As I passed the bar, I motioned for Heather to follow me. Once we were alone, I made my request. "Tomorrow night. Eight o'clock, the large play room. Grab one of the other girls, too."

Her face showed surprise, but I could tell she was excited. Too bad my enthusiasm was less about Heather and the other girl and more about fucking the thought of Ms. Pencil Skirt from my mind.

Chapter Nine

DANIELLA

y neck and back were killing me. I'd spent the last ten hours combing through Club Travesty's tax returns and looking at the books. The man kept meticulous notes; I'd give him that. But the sound of my stomach growling had me checking the time. Shit. It was past six o'clock. Where the hell was Shane? After his abrupt exit, he hadn't come back.

Just as well. Once I got into numbers, it was tough for me to get out. But I felt like I had a firm start. Tomorrow I'd start to lay out my questions for him. Since I hadn't found anything obvious missing from his returns, I would need to audit his expenditures. Auditing was normally something I'd have an on-staff auditor do. But considering the nature of this club and maybe something I didn't want to admit—me wanting to spend more time with Shane—I wasn't about to pass off the assignment to someone else.

After rolling my neck, I grudgingly put on my heels again. About five hours ago, I'd kicked them off. In search of Shane or food or maybe both, I took the front stairs down into the club.

"Wait, Miss." Lance, the man whose job I'd saved, intercepted me once I was on the main floor. Taking my arm, he led me behind the bar.

"You can't go out onto the main floor or into the bar without a mask. Unless you want to chance being recognized."

Huh. It hadn't even crossed my mind. Grateful for his quick thinking, I smiled. "Thank you. I don't suppose someone has one I could borrow."

He looked awkward. "Uh, it would be easier if you went out the back towards the employee entrance."

"Oh. I was hoping you could tell me a good place to eat around here?"

"The bar has great food. Most of the staff eats from their menu. Let me show you to the employee break room where you can place an order."

Because he was here and I felt bad I'd almost gotten him fired, I decided to say something. "By the way. I'm sorry about the other night. I never meant—"

He cut me off with a rare smile. "It's already forgotten, Ms. Trivioli."

I WAITED on my chef salad, trying my best not to gawk at the other people in the room. Most of them were gorgeous. The women, especially, were all made up and wore very little by way of clothing. Two of them were seated to my left, and I couldn't help overhearing.

"You're so lucky you're performing with Shane tomorrow night."

The blonde sighed. "More like he's performing with Heather, and I'm just along for the ride. But I'm hoping he'll let me suck that big cock of his."

I could feel my neck getting red. Jealousy wasn't an emotion with which I was familiar. Not even watching my fiancé last night have sex with other people had elicited such a response. Yet the thought of Shane with another woman was provoking a completely irrational dose of it. I shook off the crazy thought, grabbed my salad, and started to walk back upstairs. But not before snagging a menu of services.

I told myself I wanted to study the club's menu in order to follow the revenue streams more easily, but I found myself completely enthralled with the descriptions of the services offered.

As I ate my dinner, I realized I had never felt lonelier. Or more sexually frustrated. Not a great combination. Maybe it was time for a change.

SHANE

I'd stayed away from Daniella yesterday evening. Pure self-preservation. The quick answer to my problem would be to fuck her brains out and get her out of my system. But there was no way I was crossing that line. Women like her belonged in the suburbs with a white picket fence, minivan, and Pinterest habit. Not in a sex club. So why had I ensured she came back?

The question wouldn't leave my mind as I walked into my spacious loft office early the next morning. She was already at my desk, working. I immediately noticed the dark circles under her eyes and wondered about the cause.

"Good morning. Merry Christmas Eve," she greeted casually.

"'Morning. And, uh, Merry Christmas. How did you sleep?"

She appeared startled by my question but sighed when she lifted her gaze to mine. "Not great, honestly."

"Was the bed not comfortable?"

"No, it wasn't that. Maybe it's the holidays. Do you have plans with family?"

I didn't like the reminder. "No. We'll be open tonight and tomorrow. But you're welcome to take tomorrow off if you want to spend the day with yours."

"My parents are on a cruise. But they'll probably call later."

"We could, uh, do dinner later if you want?" Shit. Where had that thought come from? I didn't do holidays, family, or dinner dates.

She looked pleasantly surprised and then confused. "Uh, I thought you were performing tonight."

"Not until eight. We could eat beforehand. Or not. It doesn't matter." I disliked being put on the spot and that she was privy to my plans.

"Sure, dinner before would be nice. Is your performance up for people to watch?"

"Yes, for members. That does not include you." I added the last part in case she got any ideas.

I could feel her eyes on me as I kept mine averted.

"Why not?"

"Because I said so."

A smile curved her lips. "Funny. I haven't heard such a lame excuse since I was a child and my Dad couldn't come up with a good reason to forbid something. Do you have an issue with me watching you perform?"

I spared a glance and shouldn't have. The twinkle in her eyes was disarming. "Don't cross me on this, Daniella. You're not sneaking down there tonight."

"Give me a good reason, and maybe I won't."

"Tell me what it is you want from going down on that floor to watch."

I witnessed the color stain her cheeks while her gaze reluctantly met mine. "I don't know. Maybe just to feel something similar to the other night when you touched me."

Although she wasn't trying to seduce me, I could feel an instant pull toward her. "You're rebounding."

She blew out a frustrated breath. "Can I be brutally honest with you?"

"Of course."

"I'm not. Not rebounding, that is. And the fact that I'm more upset about being duped over the money than about losing my fiancé is disconcerting."

Her candor was disarming. "I'm gonna ask the obvious. Did you love him?"

"I hate to admit I might not have. I think I loved the idea of him. We both worked long hours, we liked the same restaurants, we ran in the same circles. It was safe and easy. But the bottom line is that when I went searching for proof about the money and cheating, I hoped I would find it."

"You wanted a way out?"

"Yeah, and how fucked up is it that I didn't simply say so? But it was in my gut. It's like I knew I wasn't destined for him."

"Not for me to judge."

"You ever been in love?"

"Nope." It was the truth. I'd been in lust a time or two, but love I didn't have time for.

"Not even when you were younger?"

I shook my head. "I never wanted the commitment."

"Anyone ever fall in love with you?"

My face flinched, and I knew she saw it. "She was young and didn't know what love was."

"Wish I could use that excuse with Eric. How about just being old and stupid?"

"You're twenty-seven. Hardly old."

"How do you know how old I am?"

"Ran your background check. I also know you've never gotten a speeding ticket, broken a law, or had bad credit."

Instead of looking annoyed, like I expected, she laughed. "Great. I'm even more boring on paper."

She stood up, coming within a breath of me. "How old are you?"

I dipped my head, whispering in her ear and enjoying the way goosebumps appeared on her flesh. "Thirty-two."

Her face was upturned when I pulled back, eyes half closed with lust. She looked as though she expected me to crash my lips to hers. When I didn't, she blinked rapidly but didn't move away. "Are you thinking about kissing me?"

"I don't kiss."

"Too personal or too boring?"

"Probably both." Kissing was what people did who had feelings for one another. The last time I'd kissed a woman, she'd misconstrued the meaning. Never again. Now when I fucked women, there wasn't a lot of time for kissing. "And in your own words, you're not looking to slum it with a sex club owner."

She crinkled her adorable brow before stepping back, breaking the moment. "That's the second time you've implied I insulted you. How? When?"

She couldn't be serious. "You said clearly you weren't so pathetic as to throw yourself at the owner of a sex club."

Her mind looked like it was rewinding and then the light of recognition dawned in her eyes. "Right, I did. Because you could have any girl you wanted. So why would I throw myself at someone like that? Meaning I'd be pathetic if I did so. Jesus. You actually thought I'd be that self-righteous?"

"You wouldn't be the first."

Her expression softened. "I'm sorry if it came across that way. My intent was self-deprecation, not to insult you."

Damn. Now I felt like shit. "I apologize for the retort about you being vanilla."

"I believe you said I was too vanilla for you ever to be

interested. Whereas my comment was a misunderstanding, I believe yours was the truth."

I pulled her close, watching as her eyes widened and her breath caught. "It wasn't the truth." I let her feel my cock hard against her in order to drive my point home. God, it would be so easy. So satisfying to sink deep inside of her. Which made it that much harder to say my next words.

"But this isn't your world, Daniella. What you need is a nice man who'll treat you well and give you two point five kids."

She pulled out of my embrace, smiling sadly before grabbing her purse. "What I need are less people thinking they know what I need. I think I'll pass on dinner tonight."

I THREW BACK the tumbler of whiskey and checked my watch. It was nearing my performance time, but I didn't feel the least bit into the thought of Heather and the other blonde—what was her name? Brandi. Damn, since when did the thought of two women leave me uninspired?

I was a complete and utter hypocrite. Even though I'd told Daniella that Club Travesty wasn't her world, I was the one who'd dragged her back into it. My reasons were purely selfish, and not entirely truthful that it had only been to do the club's books.

According to my security team, she'd returned an hour after departing and had been working upstairs. She'd probably been crying. Most likely embarrassed about having admitted she wanted to feel something more.

While walking upstairs, I tried to remind myself why I couldn't pull her into the bedroom and fuck her out of my system. That's really all it would take. One night, and I could stop obsessing about how her pussy had climaxed around my fingers. But doing so wouldn't be fair to her.

It wasn't as though I was averse to having regular sex in a bed. Ironically, the last time I'd had sex in an actual bed, I'd been twenty-two, in college, and fucking some coed who would've freaked if I'd suggested anything other than vanilla. Now I was contemplating the flavor because it had been so long I'd forgotten the taste.

God knew, I'd been involved in some kinky shit over the years. It all started when Max and I found Gloria at a bar while on vacation right after college. She was in her forties and beautiful, not in the classic sense like Daniella, but in the self-confident, sexual kind of way. And she'd introduced us to her club. Finally, we'd both felt free. Free from what society dictated, free from drunk, giggling girls at frat parties and stupid boys who didn't know how to get a woman off properly. Gloria had made sure learning to give women pleasure had been the first of her many lessons.

But now, ten years later and with the club consuming so much of my time, I found myself bored. Now that I'd been there and done most everything, I found my appetite changing. Unfortunately, it seemed to center around a certain feisty, redhead with gorgeous skin and blazing blue eyes.

When I saw she was no longer at the desk, I knocked on the bedroom door. Silence greeted me. I opened the door to find the room empty. Where the hell was she?

I turned to find Max coming off the elevator, smirking.

"Where's Daniella?"

"Not crying over your ass, that's for sure."

"What the hell is that supposed to mean?"

"It means she isn't the girl from your old neighborhood who flipped out on you and your mom because you took her out a couple of times."

I hated the reminder of Tina. She was a girl I'd met while visiting home. Though she had a rocking body, she'd gotten way too attached after a couple dates and a single night together. That mess was the reason I was now adamant about keeping things completely black and white with my partners.

"Where is she?"

"Partaking in some club activities."

Adrenaline coursed through me. I had to fight the urge to tear through each of the rooms looking for her. What the hell? This wasn't her.

"Relax, dude. She's doing the boyfriend experience with Javier. Although I was tempted to ask if she wanted it with me, I knew you'd flip out."

So much for being worried she'd get attached to me if we slept together. Obviously, that wasn't the case if she'd entertain sex with a stranger. I gritted my teeth. "What room?"

He quirked a brow. "Number five in about ten minutes. But what about your show tonight?"

Chapter Ten

DANIELLA

$\mathcal{I}$'d be damned if I'd spend the night above a sex club, frustrated and feeling sorry for myself. Especially while Shane was downstairs partaking in a jolly Christmas Eve threesome. No, thank you. There was at least one bright spot, though. The test results revealed I was clean. Eric hadn't given me anything.

Although my little confession to Shane earlier about wanting to feel something hadn't embarrassed me, what I did hate was that he saw me the same boring way I saw myself. Practical, safe and completely uninspired. But the night he'd touched me, something had changed; a craving I hadn't known existed was now unleashed. I refused to put it back into a box. So it was with a mix of anxiety and excitement that I looked forward to the 'boyfriend experience.'

"Hi, honey, how you feeling?" Cindy, one of the girls who worked at the club, walked me down the corridor. She was beautiful, with long black hair and legs for miles. A stunning tattoo winding down one of her arms had me staring. I didn't mean to, but in my dull, corporate world, I didn't see women like her.

"Okay."

"You like the ink?"

"It's beautiful. Is it a serpent?"

"It is. And on this side is a mermaid." She showed me the underside of her arm, revealing a raven-haired mermaid with a gorgeous tail.

"Now, then, this will be your room. Javier is wonderful, so you'll be in good hands."

I took a deep breath. "I hope so."

She led me into a space which surprised me. It was a beautifully decorated room with a bed in the center and a gorgeous chandelier overhead. Opulent carpet had my shoes sinking into it. In addition to the bed, there was a small sofa next to a table with refreshments.

"Are you nervous?"

She seemed pure and honest, making me truthful in my reply. "Yes. Very."

"It's understandable, but I promise Javier will ease your worries. He's very easy to talk to." She suddenly grabbed her earpiece. "Sorry, hold on."

I watched curiously as she flicked her headset. "I'm on my way." To me, she added, "I'll be right back. Have some champagne and relax."

Sure. Easy for her to say. As soon as the door closed, I had to fight the urge to flee. I also was nervous Shane would find out about this and put a stop to it. But then again, he had a performance tonight. Most likely, he wouldn't notice where I was.

What in the hell was I doing? My subconscious answered, "Having long overdue, great sex." She was hard to argue with.

Cindy came back in with an apologetic smile. "Sorry about that. Javier requested I get you ready for him."

"Ready how?"

"You should disrobe. You mentioned you wanted something kinky in the profile sheet, so I'll use silk straps to tie you to the bed and a blindfold if that's okay."

I gulped. I had said I wanted something other than plain vanilla sex. But now the thought had me nervous. "Sure. But, um, but can you make sure I can get my hands out if I need to? I'm a bit apprehensive about that part."

She nodded. "Of course. It'll be our secret."

Once I stripped out of my dress and undergarments, I found Cindy appraising me with frank interest. "You're incredibly sexy."

"Um, thank you." I climbed on the bed and once again fought my nerves.

"Here, take this. It'll help." She held out the shot glass.

I sniffed the contents, immediately identifying tequila. Bottoms up.

"Good girl."

My body started to shake against my will as Cindy fastened the silken ties above my head. I was happy she did as promised, keeping them loose enough to get out.

"Relax," she cajoled. "I'm going to rub some oil on you. It's pleasure-point heating oil."

After she poured something from a small vial, I gasped when she rubbed her hands gently over my breasts, centering on my nipples. She next held it up over my pubic area.

"Just a gentle touch. You into girls, Daniella?"

I blushed. "No. I mean you're very beautiful, but no."

She swiped her finger over my clit, teased my lips, and then went down my slit before inserting that finger into her mouth. "Too bad because you taste amazing."

Holy shit. I might not be into women, but my body definitely responded to her sexy display.

"Now with the blindfold. Remember to lie back and relax. And don't be shy with what you want. This is your fantasy, after all."

Yes. Yes, it was. But with the wrong guy. I had to fight

the urge to change my mind about this entire thing. It was now or never. By next week, I wouldn't have this opportunity.

"He's here."

I could hear the door open and shut. In that moment, I was very aware of being blindfolded.

"Okay. Um, I guess hi, Javier."

His gruff whisper came closer to me as did soft footsteps. "Hello, beautiful." It was strange how his voice seemed somewhat familiar despite the slight accent.

"Hi." My heart was pounding in my ears. "Sorry, I already said that. I'm nervous. This is the first time I've ever done something like this."

"I plan on taking good care of you."

There it was again. The eerie sensation that instead of the Spanish accent being slight, it was exaggerated. But turning to more pressing thoughts, I wondered what he thought of me on display for him. I wasn't a bombshell or anything and not very tall, but my cup size was decent, and I worked out and stayed in shape.

The oil started to heat. First I felt my nipples tingle, making them ache for someone to touch them. Then my center started pounding as if my heartbeat had replaced its location. "What is this stuff Cindy used on me?"

"It's made to stimulate your body. Now tell me, what is your fantasy?"

Shane. Thankfully, the thought stayed internal.

My mind must have been messing with me because suddenly I had a whiff of him. "Um. Something that isn't boring. Something that takes me out of my head."

"Do you have a man you're picturing?"

Was I that transparent? "Does it matter?"

"It does very much. This is where the blindfold comes in. With it, you can pretend anything you want. Now then, I'll never touch you without permission. For every touch, I will ask you beforehand. Do you want to try masturbating first? I can untie your hand."

"No. I don't have much luck with that." And something about touching myself in front of a stranger didn't turn me on.

"I'm going to massage your foot. Is that okay?"

Nope, because all of a sudden I had the skin-prickling sensation of his voice being off. I'd not yet met Javier, but that rasp belonged to only one man.

"Actually, can you start with rubbing my temples? Just to relax my mind as it's working overtime." And I hoped the nearness would give me confirmation.

"Uh. Sure."

He moved closer and suddenly was in back of me, reaching over and massaging my head gently. The familiar scent of him filled my senses. But what if Javier used the same body wash or cologne as Shane?

"Talk to me," I requested, needing more.

"You're very beautiful like this, Daniella."

Click. The way he said my name upped the likelihood of it being Shane. I was half tempted to whip off my mask to confirm, but I wanted something first, so I decided to keep the ruse.

I sucked in a breath when his warm hands traveled down to my neck and arms.

"In case you aren't enjoying something I do, beautiful, I want you to think of a safe word."

Wow. I never thought someone in this lifetime would be asking me that particular question. "Um, how about Jingle Bells?" As soon as I'd blurted it out, I cringed. Could I be any lamer with my safe words?

"Why that?"

Of course he would ask. "I don't know. Maybe because it's Christmas Eve. I can come up with another one."

"No. Jingle Bells it is. I'm going to move down to your

legs. As I get closer to your pussy, I want you to tell me green, yellow, or red. Use your safe word if you have to, which means the same thing as red."

Somehow, I thought shouting, 'Green, Green, Green' might be an instant giveaway, so I simply said, "Okay." I forced myself to relax as his hands worked up to my calves and then concentrated on my knees. But when he stroked my thighs, I shivered, anxious for more.

"Do you want me to taste you?"

"Yes, but kiss me first." I could sense his hesitation. This had to be Shane.

"On the lips?"

"Mm-hm. It's part of my fantasy."

He moved, and I could sense him above me. His lips took mine tentatively at first.

Since I could no longer help myself, I wiggled the one hand out of my restraint and wove it into his hair, pulling him deeper. The moment his tongue entered my mouth, I sucked on it, enjoying the groan emanating from his chest.

Our tongues mated, his teeth nipped, and then his mouth traveled south. He lavished attention on each breast before kissing down my stomach, hips, and then to where I practically ached for him.

I could feel his weight shift to the bed before he pushed my heels back so my legs were spread at bended knee. While he kissed my inner thighs, my legs started to shake with anticipation. His scruff running along my tender flesh had me wanting badly to flip off the mask and see his face.

At the first swipe of his tongue over my clit, I about bucked off the bed. "Jesus."

"I've been waiting to taste you."

And just like that, he dove in. Not in a way which said, hey, I'm getting to know your body, or maybe I'll tease you a bit first. But in the way that demonstrated a carnal appetite, not to mention a clear adeptness at the task. Lips, tongue, and teeth all worked together on my center of nerves to have blood roaring to my ears and then send me over the edge in seconds.

"Again," he murmured before I could recover. By adding his fingers curled up inside of me to the knuckle, he took me to the next level, one I hadn't known existed.

The one where he began fucking me with his tongue while his thumb focused on my pleasure point.

It was almost too much, this tension coiled through my body that wasn't getting a break. My mind scrambled as I was obliterated with such force that a half scream tore from my throat.

"Fuck. You come spectacularly."

The fake Javier had forgotten his accent that time.

"Must be you, Javier." I couldn't help but mess with him, wondering if he planned on giving up his disguise. I wasn't disappointed.

He climbed on the bed, his erection at my entrance, and whipped off my mask.

Time stood still and the air sizzled between us with his eyes locked on mine. A smirk came over my face while irritation took over his.

"How long did you know?"

"Long enough."

"Before the kiss?"

"Hey, you hijacked my fantasy, which included kissing. You're lucky I'm not pissed you're not Javier."

"You're lucky it wasn't him. What the hell were you thinking?"

Seriously, he was lecturing me with him on the precipice of penetration? I shifted my hips to remind him of exactly where we were. "Green, Shane."

"Fuck." He thrust into me deep on one stroke, filling me completely and holding himself still.

"Kiss me again." I leaned up, pausing a millimeter away from his lips, pleasantly amazed when he framed my face.

"Last one."

Could I help the moment of triumph? "Guess you'd better make it good, then."

He possessed my mouth while I released my second hand allowing me to move both down to grip his ass, pulling him deeper inside of me.

His tongue warred with mine. I became uninhibited in what I was taking or past the point of caring if he had set a time limit to this final kiss.

He wasn't gentle, but he wasn't overly harsh. Instead, he wavered between the two. A bite, a soft suck to soothe. And I was lost. Lost in this exquisite torture as he pumped in and out of me.

"Oh, God." I could feel it building. I closed my eyes, overwhelmed with desire.

"Open them," he demanded.

"I'm going to come."

"Look at me when you do. Don't you dare close them."

Considering he was a man who didn't want the intimacy of a kiss, having an orgasm while staring deeply into his eyes wasn't exactly impersonal. In fact, I'd never experienced anything more personal.

"Fuck," he muttered, shifting his hands to lift up my lower body. This primed it for his delicious assault of stroking my G-spot over and over until he ground out his own climax.

SHANE

Fuck was right. As in I was royally fucked that I'd let go of my boundaries with this woman. And yet I hadn't been able to help myself. The sweet taste of her lips and the surprising talent of her tongue were like a drug. If I wasn't careful, I'd become addicted.

I told myself this was only to give her the 'fantasy.' That it was a one-time thing. But as her tight cunt squeezed my cock with her orgasm, I knew one time wouldn't nearly be enough.

"You okay?" I was slick with sweat and not nearly done with her.

She unclasped her sexy legs from around my waist, allowing me to pull out.

After standing up, I disposed of the condom in the cleverly hidden trash receptacle beside the bed. I then found her eyes traveling up and down my body.

"You're gorgeous," she blurted as though unable to help herself.

"I'm glad you like what you see. Now turn over."

She raised a brow. Just when I thought she'd have a saucy reply, she instead flipped over onto her stomach, allowing me a perfect view of her heart-shaped ass.

"By the way, what happened to Javier?"

I laughed that she was just now asking. "I intercepted him and told him about the change of plans."

"I thought you had a show to do tonight."

"Max is happily filling in." I didn't want to go into why I didn't want Javier to see her like this. Touch her. Be with her. I realized the double standard as I'd been about to perform with other women.

My hands massaged her cheeks first. I enjoyed the moan of ecstasy I got when I moved the pressure to her lower back. Trailing my hand down, I played with her pussy, enjoying the slick view of it from this angle. "I wonder how far you'd have let Javier get."

"Mm, guess we'll never know."

"I think he was put out when I told him I was keeping you all to myself."

She turned so she could look at me and asked the question I was dreading. "Ah, but for how long?"

"I don't want you getting attached." It was important to me to be very clear. I didn't want a relationship. Even more critical was her comprehension of that.

Fire erupted in her eyes as I knew it would. "Maybe it's you who will get attached. Why do you assume it would be —? Oh—Oh—God, wh-what are you doing?"

I'd trailed my finger up, circling her back entrance before dipping it inside, using some of her own arousal to ease the entry. Christ, I was getting hard for her all over again.

"Has anyone had you here before?"

"No. But you're deflecting from—Wow."

I slid the fingers from my other hand into her slick heat, filling her both ways and working her gently where she'd never been touched.

"Do you like me playing with your ass, Daniella?" I added a finger, stretching her tight hole and feeling her legs start to quake. When was the last time I'd had someone innocent enough to be completely unguarded in their reaction?

"Yes."

"Say it."

She mumbled a curse before finally finding the words. "I like you—playing with my ass."

"Come for me you, dirty girl. Come hard." After curling my fingers up into her pussy while pumping her ass, I was rewarded with a gush that even took me off guard. Holy shit, my girl could come.

Now where the fuck had that dangerous thought come from? But before I could analyze it, she'd sat up. She slid so she was on the edge of the bed, legs spread around the outside of my thighs and face flushed from the orgasm I'd given her.

"What else is your fantasy for one night?" I murmured the words, wanting to give her the best time of her life.

"You. Everywhere. In my mouth, in my pussy, and in my ass."

I froze. How did a girl go from not getting a proper orgasm to wanting me to fuck her in every possible place? "Jesus."

She nipped at my ear. "Don't tell me I've shocked you?"

"A little surprised, that's all. But I'd hurt you if I had your ass tonight. You need to be prepped properly for your first time." I might not be an overly sensitive lover, but I wasn't completely without regard for my partner and her well-being.

She slid down off the table and onto her knees, taking a hold of my length. "Then just the other two."

Holy fuck. Who was this insatiable creature in front of me?

Chapter Eleven

DANIELLA

I'm not sure what had come over me, but I was suddenly a woman starved at a time-limited, all-you can-eat buffet. And I was getting my money's worth. Which was a really shitty metaphor since it made Shane a hooker. I guessed he wouldn't appreciate that, but I simply couldn't get enough.

I concentrated on the fully erect—Wowsers, that was a great cock in front of me. Thick, long, hard, and standing at attention as though he hadn't fucked me senseless just moments ago. And the body it belonged to. Holy hell. Like a sinful dream, he was cut and corded in muscles in all the right places.

He looked a bit taken aback that I'd dropped to my knees. I enjoyed putting that look on his face. The look which said *holy shit what is this woman doing to me*. Yes, indeed. I planned for him to wear that expression the rest of the evening.

After licking the pre-cum from the tip, I teased it for a moment before swallowing him whole to the back of my throat. I might not have a lot of talent or experience in the bedroom, but I'd discovered something when going down on my first guy in college. I'd been blessed by the blow job gods with no gag reflex.

"Christ, Daniella."

It was music to my ears to hear a man like Shane say those words as if he couldn't help himself. "Mmm," I hummed, using my tongue to lubricate him while I gripped his base and then eased to the tip before swallowing him down again.

"Fuuuuuuuuuuuuck."

Sucking the tip, I gave him a few pumps with my hand. "Am I doing something you don't like?"

He grinned and looked down, appearing half stunned and half amused. "Not even close, sweetheart. But here I thought I'd have to give you tips or something. I was very wrong."

After teasing the crown and mouthing the head, I took him back down, forcing myself to breathe through my nose and relaxing my throat all the way. Gripping his impressively muscled ass, I bobbed on his length for a moment before realizing he was hesitating.

"Fuck my mouth, Shane." Which kind of came out garbled because, you know—dick in my mouth and all. But he'd understood it enough to grip my hair and start to thrust.

"You're gonna make me come. Tap me now if you don't want it deep."

The fact he was considerate enough to warn me made me want him even more. And when the first drop of salty cum hit my tongue, I found myself greedy for the taste. Greedy to swallow it all down. I capped it off with a slow lick from his base to the tip to ensure I got every last drop.

I looked up to see his shocked face.

"Where did you learn to do that?"

Smirking, I rose to my feet with a hand from him and then shrugged. "No gag reflex wasn't really learned, but it does seem to get the boys excited."

It was meant as a joke, but given the way his eyes darkened and the scowl etched on his face, I knew he wasn't taking it as such. Then it was his turn to shock me when he gripped my hair and put his fingers back inside of me.

"You shouldn't be thinking about anyone but me," he growled in my ear and proceeded to kiss down the column of my neck.

His possessive tone surprised me but not as much as it turned me on. "Then make sure I don't."

SHANE

As a rule I didn't sleep with a woman. As in fall asleep, cuddle, or stay until morning. Which is why it felt foreign to wake up with Daniella curled up next to me, her head on my chest, hair splayed over my shoulder, and legs entwined with mine. I told myself it was out of consideration that I didn't wake her right away. In truth, I knew the moment I left this bed, whatever magic had started last night and bled into the wee hours would be gone.

One night. It's what I'd been willing to give, and what she'd been willing to settle for. So then, why was I hesitating in getting up?

Extricating myself slowly, I moved from the bed and stood at the side looking down at her. She was stunning, with her flawless skin and beautiful lashes which framed the prettiest blue eyes I'd ever seen. And her entirely fuckable naked body was doing nothing for the little bit of resolve I still had to keep things at one night. I wanted more than anything to slide into her warmth and bring her to climax all over again.

I pulled on my slacks before I could give in to the temptation, telling myself I was doing the right thing. Since the cleaning crew would be coming in bright and early, I couldn't leave her in one of the sex rooms to wake up. So I slipped on my shirt and shoes, gathered her things, and settled on simply wrapping her in a sheet.

There probably wouldn't be anyone about this time of morning, especially on Christmas Day, but I didn't want to take any chances.

She hardly stirred in my arms when I gathered her to me and lifted her off the bed. Earlier, she'd practically passed out after I'd fucked her into so many orgasms I'd lost count. God, this girl could come. Her body was a treasure chest of ways to make her climax.

I carried her out the door and down the hall to the elevator, not passing a single person yet knowing it was all on the security cam. Not that my guys would ever let on. Discretion was our business.

After taking her up to the bed, I set her gently in the middle of it, sighing with regret at letting her go. She stirred slightly but then curled up under the warmth of the blankets.

I had to fight the physical temptation to join her. The only thing that kept me from doing so was the fear that I'd send the wrong message—in neon.

I SLEPT a couple of hours at my loft apartment a few blocks away before returning to the club. Luckily, I didn't need a lot of sleep to operate. Just some coffee, of which I grabbed a cup for Daniella, too. I was hoping to cut the awkwardness I was sure would be present this morning when I first saw her.

Scenarios floated through my head about how it would go, but ultimately, I knew if she brought up wanting another night, I'd have to let her down easy.

But when I went up the stairs, instead of finding her alone and waiting on me, I saw she had her suitcase in hand and was smiling up at Max.

Chapter Twelve

DANIELLA

I woke up in bed wondering how the hell I'd gotten there. At least it was still on the early side. If the lack of clothing didn't tip me off that my night with Shane had been real, then the fact I was sore pretty much everywhere confirmed it.

I got up, showered, and pulled myself together. I couldn't help grinning at the way my night had turned out. But then reality set in. At least a week's worth of work remained where I had to be around the man. Taking a deep breath, I resolved not to be weird or clingy. I'd had a night I'd never forget. In fact, I wondered if any other man would be able to measure up to the experience. But the time to dwell on that fear would be later, once I was out of Shane's world and didn't have to see him every day.

Since I was hoping there would be availability in the hotel next door, I called and was happy to snag an open room. So the first order of business was to pack my things and get my own space. As I lugged my suitcase out to the office, I felt lucky to find Max there, sipping coffee at his desk.

"Where ya going?"

"Next door to the hotel."

He arched a brow. "Shane know?"

My face scrunched up, expressing my confusion as to why it would matter. "It was the plan all along."

He relaxed some and got to his feet, giving me his trademark grin. "All right. Let me help you."

"What in the hell is going on here?"

Shane's tone and appearance had me at a loss for words.

Luckily, Max didn't have the same trouble. "Daniella is moving next door to the hotel. Why don't I go get you checked in and, uh, give you two some privacy?"

Shane simply stood there staring at me until Max disappeared into the elevator heading down. "Why are you moving out?"

"We agreed. The hotel had an opening today. And I thought to give you your room back."

He moved closer, stopping only a breath away from me. "And it has nothing to do with last night?"

"No, why would it?" I hated the fact my voice went down to an involuntary whisper.

"Not very convincing." His voice was husky, his eyes intense.

I took a deep breath, far too affected by his presence for my health. This only emphasized why I needed my own space. "It was the original plan, and after last night, I think it might be better to have a separation."

He lifted a brow. "Are you still okay with working here?"

"Of course."

My conviction must've rung true as he stepped back. "Okay. Good. How's it going so far?"

I tried not to take it personally that he might be anxious to be rid of me. "All right. I plan on working every day until the New Year except for Sunday. I have a wedding to attend."

The wedding was for my cousin, who happened to be

marrying Eric's former roommate. Although the last thing I wanted was to see Eric in a social setting, I'd already sent an RSVP and felt an obligation to go. Wasn't like it was their fault my ex-fiancé was a douche bag.

Shane and I both turned when Heather came up the stairs, calling out. It was a simple reminder that we were never alone in this space.

"Hey, Shane. Oh, hi. You're not alone. I can come back."

He frowned. "No, it's fine. You've met Daniella, right?"

She gave me a half-assed smile. Upon meeting me yesterday, she hadn't been overly friendly. Obviously, that didn't change even in her boss's presence.

"Yep, we met. You have a minute?"

Damn. I was being dismissed. "Uh, I can come back."

"No, stay. We'll go." He moved towards Heather.

I heard her ask in a voice that was unmistakably meant to be overheard, "Do we have a raincheck for tonight, lover?"

Damn. Perhaps it was time to work extra hours to get done with this job because, now that we'd been together, the thought of Shane with anyone else made my stomach turn.

IT WAS after nine o'clock at night on Christmas Day, but still I worked. I was determined to get through my first two years of an audit that would go back a total of five. The good news was it was all reconciling. The bad news was that I wasn't sure my work was the only reason I was here so late. Sure, I was known to work long hours, but I admitted to myself I was still here tonight out of morbid curiosity. I wanted to see if Shane would be partaking in the night's show.

I hadn't seen him during the remainder of the day. Although Max had long ago given me the key to my hotel room next door, I hadn't moved from my spot at the desk.

The exception was a late lunch, when I couldn't ignore the hunger pains any longer and had taken a break to grab a burger from the bar.

Unable to stand the uncertainty of whether or not Shane was down below in one of the playrooms, I shut my laptop down and put everything in my bag. This way if I did see him, I could leave quickly. Taking a deep breath, I went over to the door that I assumed led to the viewing room where one could see down below. I don't know if I was relieved or not when the handle turned, allowing me access.

A quick glance showed me the room was empty. The couch and two chairs made it the perfect 'box suite' to watch all of the action below. I stepped close to the glass and glanced down. There were quite a few people, although nothing close to how many had attended the Christmas party.

My breath caught at the sight of a very well-muscled man standing naked in the center of the room. There were two women placed on their knees: one in front of him, her hand wrapped around his massive erection and one in back, kneading and kissing his firm buttocks. Surely she wasn't going to— Holy shit. She was. Both women literally dove into their front and back door tasks while the man threw back his head in complete ecstasy.

"Do you like to watch, Daniella?"

Jesus. I nearly jumped out of my skin at the sound of Shane's voice. When I attempted to turn, he wasn't having it.

"Face forward and tell me."

I licked my lips. "I find myself fascinated with it all."

His breath came at my neck, and I had to resist the urge to turn around and throw myself on him.

"Why did you come in here tonight?"

I didn't bother to lie. "I wondered if you would be down there."

"If I had been, would you have stayed to watch me?"

"No."

His fingers undid my bun, letting my hair fall down my back. "Does this turn you on, to watch the man down there with two women on their knees pleasuring him?"

"With you here, yes."

"Put your hands up against the glass."

"What?" I attempted to turn around, only to have his hard body crowd my space.

"I said, place your hands on the glass. And spread your legs."

My shaking hands took purchase on the window while I widened my stance slightly, wondering what in the hell he had planned. Unable to help myself, I asked, "What are you doing?"

A shudder ran through my body when his hands cupped my backside.

"Admiring your black dress and the way it hugs your curves."

"I thought the agreement was only last night." Not that I was complaining, but my mind struggled to keep up with both my body's agenda and now his.

"What if we said twenty-four hours instead?" His fingers had slipped between my legs and under the crotch of my panties.

"Yes. Twenty-four hours." Although, technically, it was past that. I cursed my stupid brain for numbers and told it to shut the hell up.

"You're so wet. Were you this way while watching Philip below?"

"No. Only once I heard your voice."

"Good girl."

A sharp tug and the sound of material ripping meant I was rid of my thong.

"I want you to watch the show while I fuck you."

My eyes, which had been closed, focused back on the

scene in front of me. The players had now moved to the bed where Philip had one woman riding him while the other literally sat on his face. "Shane." I moaned his name when fingers entered me. I could hear the sound of a package being ripped open and soon after was practically lifted up when he entered me on one stroke.

"You're tight. You're not too sore, are you?" He hesitated, clearly waiting to thrust again.

Although I was a little tender, there was no way I was stopping now. "That ship has sailed. Fuck me."

He gripped my hair and pulled out only to slam back in. "Like this? Tell me if this is too rough."

"No, it's not. God." He set a furious pace and, as I started to build, he reached around to rub my clit. The orgasm hit me like a freight train. A string of unintelligible words ripped from my throat as the rush started at my toes and didn't seem to be stopping. Because neither was Shane.

"I can't," I mumbled, losing any strength I'd had in bracing myself against the glass. Boneless, I allowed him to turn me around, lift me up, and push my entire back flush with the wall before entering me again. My hands gripped his powerful shoulders while my legs wrapped around him. If I'd had a brain cell to spare, I would've marveled at the fact he could hold me up as though I was nothing. But I was too lost in the pleasure to think.

"Yes. Right there." He'd found the spot and increased the pace until I was coming spectacularly, raking my nails over his back while he buried himself deep and growled in my ear.

"Your pussy is like a vice grip demanding I come with you."

"Mm. I quite like that."

He walked me over to the couch and, after pulling out, let me down easy. I watched while he expertly removed the condom and tied it off. He put it into a small trash can over by the bar area to one side.

"You're welcome to spend the night in your room here."

"Are you spending it with me?" The question was part curious, part challenge.

He came over and helped me up, his arm banding around my waist, eyes on mine. "It wouldn't be a good idea."

"No. I suppose not. Good night, then."

"Good night."

And yet he didn't move. Neither did I. The temptation to lean in to kiss him was so strong I swore he could actually read my mind because he stepped back. "I'll walk you out."

The gesture surprised me, but I was grateful he led the way down the stairs and out the employee entrance to the hotel lobby next door.

"What room are you in?"

I fished the card from my bag with the number on it. "It's on the eleventh floor. Eleven fifteen."

He didn't hesitate to put his hand at the small of my back and lead me into the elevator, pressing my floor. I turned to him once the doors closed. "You don't have to see me up."

"I know." His handsome poker face gave nothing away.

We walked down the hall in silence until we reached my number. I swiped my key and opened the door to a beautiful junior suite with my suitcase in the quaint seating area.

He came in and glanced around. "I hope everything is to your liking."

I nodded. "It's nice, although you didn't have to spring for a suite."

"It wasn't me; it was Max."

"Oh." Awkward.

"So, uh, I'll see you in the morning." Suddenly, he appeared anxious to leave.

"Yep. I finished two years' worth today and will start again tomorrow." I wasn't sure why I felt this was the moment to tell him what my work plan was, but it came out before I could help myself. Perhaps it was to serve as a reminder of why I was really here.

He moved towards the door. "Great. Uh. Merry Christmas."

Yeah. Merry Christmas. It had certainly been a strange one.

Chapter Thirteen

SHANE

I don't know what I'd been thinking tonight except I that had to have her. Had to possess her the moment I saw her at the window looking down at the scene with wide eyes. Then it had gotten awkward, with me taking her up to her hotel room only to say goodnight.

There'd been something about her curiosity regarding what was happening in the rooms and then her honesty about being turned on the moment I'd stepped behind her. But I was flirting with a dangerous line. Hell, using the excuse of twenty-four hours had been a flimsy one. As a result, instead of quelling my desire for her, I'd kicked it up another notch.

But tomorrow was a new day and a new resolve. I was a man of discipline, so keeping Daniella at arm's length shouldn't be a problem.

Until I walked in the next morning to see her in a fire-engine red dress, librarian glasses, and an infuriatingly sexy updo that made me want to rip it out and run my fingers through it.

She looked up smiling. "Oh, good. You're here. I need to ask you some questions about the bar inventory. I don't have all of the receipts."

"You can talk to Heather about anything you need regarding the bar." I regretted my gruff tone the minute her smile disappeared.

"Okay. Will do." She went back to the laptop, ready to ignore me.

"How many more days do you think you'll be here?"

She glared at me before standing up, clear annoyance in her body language. "I'm working as fast as I can, twelve-hour days. I estimate I'll be done by the beginning of next week, although if you're thinking I'm not working fast enough, then by all means, I'll pack my shit and go."

That fire was the undoing of everything I'd convinced myself last night should hold true. "I wasn't criticizing your work ethic."

"Then what?"

Chad the bouncer's voice broke the moment. He'd apparently come up the stairs behind me. "Boss, we have a situation with one of the deliveries out back."

"I'll be there in a minute." I heard his retreating footsteps and closed the gap between Daniella and me in two strides. I cupped her face. "We'll talk later."

"About what?"

I smirked, a litany of dirty thoughts running through my head. "About you taking off your panties and working here all morning while I think about your bare pussy under your dress and prepare to take a long lunch when I can fuck you."

Her breath caught, and I could see the arousal reflected in her expression. So her words took me off guard. "Twenty-four hours is up."

I stroked her face. "Guess we'll have to negotiate something else, then."

DANIELLA

It was nearly two hours after Shane had said he wanted to negotiate something else, and I sat at my desk staring unseeingly at my computer screen. I didn't know whether his arrogance was a turn-on or an irritation. If I was being honest with myself, it was a bit of both. The moment he'd walked in this morning, my body, the traitor it was becoming, had reacted to him. Then he'd been a dick, but instead of turning me off, it had only upped the ante.

Even I wasn't fool enough not to recognize I was out of my depth with a man like Shane. This was why I was adamant I not become anxious for his affection. I had more self-respect than that. Not to mention that as good as it felt to be with him, I couldn't help challenging him.

But then he'd gone and thrown me for a loop by saying we would be negotiating something else. Why? It was the first question that came to mind. In a world where he could go downstairs and have any woman he wanted, women with far more experience and who were far more sexy, why did he want me? I wasn't the insecure type, but I was logical in asking the obvious question.

Annoyed at myself at losing time over the distraction and the anticipation of Shane's return, I jumped when Max's question brought me out of my thoughts.

"How's it going, Daniella?"

"Good. Although I need to go talk to Heather about the bar inventory, unless you think you can help." I was hopeful he could assist me with avoiding her.

He grinned. "Afraid not. But Heather is pretty on top of things. She should be able to answer all your questions."

"I'll go down there in a bit."

"Psyching yourself up for it?"

I had to laugh. "She doesn't care for me, and I have no clue why, so, yeah."

He quirked a brow. "You don't know why?"

"And you do?"

He chuckled. "Let's just say Heather has long had a thing for Shane even though she's tried to hide that it's anything more than physical. And him standing her up the other night in order to be with you didn't win you any favors."

Ah. "Wait, but she was with you. Isn't that, uh, offensive?"

Now he was really grinning. "I don't take offense at much."

He must not.

"And good luck with Heather."

I DECIDED NOT to put off inquiring about the receipts any longer. I went downstairs to find the longtime bar manager. She was doing inventory in the back with two other guys who were helping her move some things.

"Hey, Heather," I said from the doorway.

She turned at the sound of my voice and then went back to her task without so much as a smile or a welcome.

"Shane said you would have the detailed bar records from the last few years."

That got her attention and earned me a glare. "What of it?"

"As you're probably aware, I'm doing an audit of the last five years. In order to do that, I need to go through the ledger and all the receipts."

"I keep meticulous records."

"Great. If you could give me the last five years, I'll be able to complete the audit on the bar."

Her eyes raked over me from head to toe, a less-than-nice smirk on her face. "You do realize you're only a fad to him, right?"

I checked my temper and tried not to look around at the two guys who were obviously watching our exchange. "I'm only here speaking with you about the receipts, not asking for unsolicited advice."

"It wasn't advice, honey. It's a warning. Shane doesn't get attached. You're just a new piece of ass for a short time before he goes back to what he knows."

Implying her. "Then think of it as incentive to get me the receipts quickly. Because the quicker I have them, the faster I finish and the faster I'm gone."

With those parting words, I turned on my heel.

Chapter Fourteen

SHANE

*I*n a place like this, the rumor mill runs rampant. That's why I waited until later that evening to approach Daniella. Somehow I knew I wouldn't find her in the best of moods after the exchange with Heather I'd heard about. What I found most impressive was how Daniella had kept her cool with Heather.

I found her poring over her notebook, an adorable little frown on her face as she crunched the numbers with a pen between her lips.

"You trying to get out of here sooner by working late nights?"

She glanced up and then back toward her book. "Considering how often people keep asking when I'm leaving, I'd say it's in everyone's interest to get this done quickly."

"Not everyone. Did you lose the panties?" If I was a betting man, I'd say she absolutely hadn't.

"What do you think?" She finally put down her pen, stood up, and focused fully on me.

I walked towards her, stopping a breath away from her. "I think if I were to reach up under your dress, I'd find cotton."

She smirked. "Satin, but yes."

"Ah, but the question is would it be wet?"

"What are we doing, Shane?"

This wasn't a question I was familiar with hearing, let alone answering. But then again, Daniella was the type of woman I was normally avoided. Yet here I was, about to step into dangerous territory. "Redefining our timeframe." I brushed my fingertips down the column of her neck, feeling her shiver at my touch.

"To what end?"

This was the part about which I needed to be absolutely clear. Not only did I want to ensure things didn't get messy, but I also wasn't a complete asshole and didn't want to give her the wrong impression. I'd made that mistake when I was younger and hurt someone who'd fancied herself in love with me. "The same end it would have been if this was still yesterday morning."

She sucked in a breath when my hand moved up her dress, stroking her inner thigh. "I think I'm having déjà vu from our first time."

I smiled in remembrance, brushing my knuckle over the soaked material. "I do believe I was behind you, loving the way your ass fit perfectly against me."

She leaned in. "Does this new arrangement include kissing?"

I shook my head, partly regretful because she was a great kisser.

"Too intimate?"

"I don't want any misunderstandings. This isn't a relationship, a start of one, or anything resembling one."

"Thank fuck, because the last thing I want is another one right now."

I threw my head back and laughed at her unexpected words. Then I got serious, cupping her chin. "What do you want, then?"

She smiled. "You. And although I'm okay with the no kissing, I'm not okay with sharing."

"Monogamy without kissing. That's a new one."

Her gasp was like music to my ears when I moved her thong to the side and plunged a finger deep inside of her.

"Think of it as short-term exclusivity. I realize in your position that might make things difficult, but oh—oh, God."

I didn't let her finish her thought, instead curling my fingers up and bringing her to orgasm, loving the rush of wetness coating my fingers and running down her thighs.

"Now, what were you saying?"

"I—Jesus. I can't even remember my own name at the moment."

A satisfied smile curved my lips. "I'll agree to only you and me for the short term. Considering everything I have planned, neither of us would have time for anyone else."

"Mm, 'kay."

I grinned at her post-orgasmic answer, walked her into the bedroom, and made quick work of having her naked and writhing beneath me under the tutelage of my fingers. But I wasn't done by a mile, choosing to go south and stay there for the next thirty minutes until I brought her orgasm count to five.

"I can't. I can't possibly have any more," she panted.

I swiped at her clit again with my tongue before relenting and kissing up her flat stomach, marveling at how soft her skin was.

"I bet you can because I'm not even close to being done."

DANIELLA

The next morning I awoke naked and alone with one thought.

Jesus, the man had stamina.

Not to mention a very sophisticated skill set regarding bringing a woman to orgasm. When he'd said he wasn't close to being done, it turned out he was a man of his word. Even after fucking me doggy style until I collapsed into a heap on the bed, unable to support myself any longer, he hadn't been finished. He'd then positioned me on top of him, my back to his front, and strummed me like a cello while he continued to thrust into me from below. Although I normally had a head for numbers, I couldn't keep track of the tally of orgasms he'd given me over the hours.

Yes. Hours. That much I'd learned from looking at the clock once I'd collapsed, completely spent. As much as I knew it would be most prudent to return to my hotel room to sleep, I could hardly move and had fallen asleep where I lay.

Without another choice now that it was morning, I donned the dress I'd worn yesterday. I slipped out to find Max eating cereal at his desk.

He looked up with a smirk. "Walk of shame?"

I quirked a brow. "I have nothing to feel ashamed about, so no."

He grinned. "Atta girl. You want some Lucky Charms?"

I laughed. "No, thank you. Uh, I guess have a good night."

"More like morning. It's five o'clock."

I yawned as if on cue. "Damn. Guess I'll see you in a couple hours."

"See ya then."

SHIT. I'd overslept. Was it any wonder, though? I slipped out of bed sore yet at the same time very satisfied. I took a quick shower, put my hair up in a high ponytail, and settled for a simple blue shift dress.

Since I was already running late, I took an extra ten

minutes to grab coffee before walking next door. It wasn't like I had an actual start time, although pushing ten o'clock in the morning seemed late for any work day.

I had just sat down at Shane's desk when I heard the footsteps on the stairs. I looked up to see him looking absolutely drool worthy in a dark gray suit with a black tie on a crisp white shirt.

"You're late."

I took a sip of coffee, defiance emanating in my slow drink. "I was unaware we set a start time."

He moved closer, stopping on the other side of the desk and leaning in so I could smell him. Damn. I already craved him again. His suit wasn't helping. I wanted to rip it off.

"Why are you late?"

I wasn't about to let him have the satisfaction of telling him he'd worn me out last night. "Long line at Starbucks."

He grinned and then straightened, taking something out of his pocket. "Stand up and bend over the desk."

"Pardon?" He couldn't mean here and now, could he?

"I'm pretty sure you heard me, Dani. If you expect me to take your ass, we need to work you in."

SHANE

Despite the shock evident on her beautiful face with her wide eyes and parted lips, I could spot the tell-tale signs of arousal my blunt words had produced by the pink on her cheeks and her quickened breath.

Considering I'd left her with reluctance in the wee hours, I was now unable to resist touching her a moment longer. I moved behind her and coaxed her to a standing position. Banding my arm around her waist, I breathed in her ear and enjoyed the shiver caused by my words.

"Put your hands on the desk and bend over."

"But anyone could come up here." Her protest came at the same time as her compliance.

"Then we need to be quick." My hand snaked up her dress, only to come in contact with her thong. "From now on, no panties while you're working here. Every morning and every lunch hour, I'm going to bend you over and ah— You're so fucking wet for me, aren't you?"

Her breath caught at the sweet intrusion of my fingers. I would never tire of the way she responded to me. Like it was the first time every time.

"You do seem to have that effect on me."

I trailed the pad of my thumb over her most sensitive spot, so very tempted to give her what her body craved, but she was right. Anyone could come up at any time, and I knew Daniella would be mortified if we were caught. Which meant I had limited time. I took the cylinder butt plug out of my pocket and loved the fact I wouldn't need the lube. Instead, I slid it into her heat.

"Holy shit. What is that?"

I pulled it out of her pussy and slid it backward, setting it in place in her pucker and gently pushing it in. "It's the smallest size plug. You'll wear it until this afternoon and then I'll take it out. Tomorrow, we'll do it with one that's larger."

"It feels strange. How am I supposed to sit down?"

I chuckled, removing my hand. "You'll manage."

She straightened up and turned with temper written all over her expression. "That's it? You're just going to tease me and leave me with this?"

"Indeed I am. And don't even think about touching yourself."

She rolled her eyes. "As if that's ever worked."

Damn. As if I wasn't hard enough, a vision sprang to mind of her playing with herself while I watched and taught her how to give herself an orgasm.

Her gaze wandered down and a smirk came to rest on her

perfect lips. "I see I'm not the only one affected. I'm assuming the same rules apply?"

Actually, I'd planned on jerking off. "You positive you're prepared if I abide by the same rule? Might be better for me to take the edge off."

She lifted a brow. "Challenge accepted."

I chuckled, framing her face, and not quite knowing what the hell I was doing. If it wasn't for Heather's voice, I might have kissed her perfect, pouty lips.

"Shane, are you ready to go?"

I didn't miss the way Daniella's body stiffened at the interruption. "Yeah. I'll meet you downstairs."

I didn't break contact until Heather's footsteps retreated, and then I dropped my hands from Daniella's face.

She surprised me by reaching up to straighten my tie. It was an intimate gesture which suddenly had me in a hurry to put some space between us.

"I dig the suit, by the way."

"You would. Sort of gives the impression I'm an actual business man."

She sighed as she tightened the knot, not letting me go. "Whatever you need to tell yourself so you can keep your barriers up. Maybe when you're with your bar manager on the way to the meeting, you can tell her to get me her receipts. Without them, one has to wonder if you've found your problem for missing revenue right there."

I disliked her implication regarding either statement. "Don't let your jealousy cloud your judgment. Heather has been a hell of an employee for ten years."

Her eyes blazed, but she simply stepped back and took her seat. "Then providing the receipts should be an easy task for her."

Chapter Fifteen

SHANE

$\mathcal{I}$ didn't like that she'd called me on my shit about keeping my barriers up. There was only one person who made a habit of doing so. Max. I also didn't care for her tone about Heather. But considering that once Heather got into my car to drive to Jersey for our meeting, she tried to dive into my lap, I could see where the jealousy stemmed from.

"Not today, honey." I tried to let her down easy, but she wasn't taking no for an answer.

Using a tone which instantly grated on my nerves, she whined, "But it's been forever, and then you stuck me with Max the other night. Are you not attracted to me anymore?"

This was the shit I tried to avoid with females. There was no right answer aside from the words she was looking for, which was to allow her to suck me off in the car. What I was about to say would make my life a whole lot more complicated, but it was the truth.

"I've got something going on with Daniella."

As predicted, this went over like a cum shot in the eye. "So, what? Now, all of a sudden, you do relationships?"

"Enough. My personal business is just that. We've always

maintained a professional working friendship, Heather, and I would hate for this to come between us."

She stewed on my warning for a few seconds.

Because I was tired of the shit she was giving Daniella in doing her job, I made myself clear. "Also, give her the receipts she requested."

Heather glanced my way, about to open her mouth, but the look I gave her stifled whatever she was about to say.

It was good to know I hadn't lost my touch on most women, making them recognize when I meant business.

"Fine."

———

I'D AVOIDED Daniella until later than planned. I could tell myself it wasn't because she had my number about my defense mechanisms or it wasn't because I was pissed the entire bar now knew I was in some sort of relationship with her—thanks to Heather's big mouth. But the truth was that all of it had me feeling out of sorts. And I didn't do out of sorts. I did control. And I did it well. Until recently, that is.

If I'd been a wise man, I would've marched up my steps to my office and told her this arrangement was off. Instead, I stood there watching her type away on her laptop, poring over the receipts Heather must've finally provided.

Sensing my presence, she glanced up briefly but then went back to work.

Huh. Not being a man who typically garnered this type of reaction from a woman, I wasn't sure what to do. "I take it you got the receipts from Heather."

She lifted her eyes, slid off her glasses, and met my gaze as I walked towards her. "Indeed. I'm guessing the thanks should go to you?"

Her tone was cool, professional even, but her eyes were anything but. They reflected her temper.

"None necessary. It should've been done sooner."

"Right. Glad you could discuss that—and our arrangement—in the car ride with her."

Ah. So that was the irritation. "It was either tell her we had a thing going on or let her suck my dick along the way."

Although I wasn't known for my filter, now would've probably been the time to exercise one. She was up and gathering her stuff, turning off the desk lamp and clearly ready to leave. "Good night, Shane."

Fuck. "Wait. Look, don't be mad. She made a move, and I shut her down. I don't get why it would piss you off."

"What pisses me off is I've had this plug up my ass all day with a promise of this afternoon, which you conveniently forgot about. I'm not well versed in the rules of anal etiquette, but that just seems straight-up rude."

My brows shot sky high. "You still have it in?"

She threw up her hands. "Seriously? What the hell was I supposed to do with it?"

No wonder she was cranky. I had to bite my lip to keep from laughing or else she'd give me a well-deserved punch in the face.

"I'm sorry. You should've taken it out. Just a couple hours a day, not eight hours."

Her face was beet red, and I found it adorable.

"Great. Now I'm going to have a big gaping you know what."

The fact she couldn't say asshole had uncontrollable laughter bubbling up from inside of me. This, of course, only served to turn her a brighter shade of red and piss her off.

"Come here." I pulled in her close to me, wrapping her up in my arms and breathing in her signature scent of something light and floral. "I'm sorry. It may not seem this way, but I'm not laughing at you. I'm only completely and totally enthralled by the combination of your humor and innocence."

I leaned back and tucked her hair behind her ear. "It makes me want to know what you're thinking all the time."

"Right now I'm thinking I'm a butt plug failure."

We both erupted into a fit of laughter together.

Max interrupted, looking completely amused to find us both giggling like starry-eyed lovers in an embrace.

"Uh, sorry to intrude, but, uh, we have a situation down in room four I need your help with."

Shit. "I need to—"

"Go on. It'll give me time to, uh, take care of things."

I chuckled, wishing like hell I could help.

DANIELLA

I took care of business by way of removing the plug. For the record, this wasn't as sexy as when Shane had put it in. Then I took a shower, hoping he would join me any minute. Then, because he hadn't, I went into the viewing room. I hoped I could see what might be going on with room four. But other than two couples having group sex, I didn't see anything out of the ordinary. Since when did four people having group sex become normal? Evidently, the club and Shane had changed my expectations.

"Whatcha doing in here?"

I spun around to see the object of my thoughts. Despite looking hot as ever, his eyes were tired. It seemed he was never "off" of work.

"Looking for you. What happened?"

He sighed. "Someone got too rough. It doesn't occur often, but unfortunately, it does happen. It gets tricky because often-times an untrained submissive doesn't recognize their limit. Even worse, an untrained dominant doesn't always know how to use some of the devices."

My jaw about dropped. I'd obviously guessed kinky stuff

happened here, but I hadn't thought about it from that perspective. "Any liability for your club?"

He shook his head. "There's always a possibility, but we do make them sign waivers. Plus, we asked if she wanted to press charges and ensured she did not. Matter of fact, they left together, so I'm assuming they'll work out whatever happened."

Not for the first time, I wondered if I was barely scratching the surface of sexually satisfying a man like Shane. "Are you into that sort of stuff?"

He smirked. "Why? You thinking you might want to try to be submissive?"

I scrunched up my nose. "I don't think I'd make a very good one. Most likely, you bossing me around would piss me off within minutes."

He moved closer, grasping my waist with his hands. "You enjoy me being bossy."

A smile curved my lips. "True. But I'm not really into pain for pleasure."

"Says the girl who had a plug up her ass most of the day."

I grinned. "I was told the end result would be worth it."

He stepped into me, dipping his lips to my ear. "Oh, it will be. You'll come so hard you'll nearly pass out from it."

Yes, please. "Mm, and when is this happening?"

"Sunday night. You'll wear a bigger one tomorrow in preparation."

I sighed. "I won't be here. I have a wedding to go to."

"What wedding?"

"The one I told you about the other day. It's my cousin, which means I can't back out."

He didn't mince words. "Sounds dreadful."

At least I had a sexy dress to wear. In fact, I looked pretty damn good in the black strapless Vera Wang dress. "It will be, especially if Eric shows up which, knowing him, he probably will."

"Did he pay you half the money?"

I nodded. "Yep. Wired as directed. He has two more weeks for the other half. You know, I don't even know if our friends have heard we broke up."

That was weird. I mean, normally, didn't a woman, upon realizing her fiancé was cheating, call her friends, have a girls' night, and cry on their shoulders? I could say I hadn't wanted to bother anyone during the holidays—which is why we'd done the whole shower and bachelorette party weeks ago. But the truth was that I'd been enveloped in the club and Shane so quickly that the whole tragedy had sort of slipped my mind.

He quirked a brow. "You didn't tell anyone about the breakup?"

"Um, I guess I forgot." Was it any wonder? Since Eric's betrayal, I'd been absolutely consumed with either the man in front of me or his taxes. "My parents were out of town. Matter of fact, I think they returned today from their cruise."

Crap. I guess I should call them since we'd only traded voicemails on Christmas. I dreaded having to do so. My mom would make my breakup with Eric a reflection of my inability to make a good wife. She'd then bring up the whole not-wanting-to-have-kids thing again. Evidently in her mind, my lack of desire to procreate made me somehow less worthy of love and marriage.

"Huh."

I frowned. "What do you mean 'huh'?"

"Sometimes people don't tell others about a breakup because they hope to maybe work things out."

I couldn't help laughing. There was no part of me wanting to work it out with Eric. "That is not happening. Not only is he a thief, but also a cheater. Normally people are upset by a breakup instead of feeling freed, so maybe that's why I haven't told anyone. Because I realize it was a mistake to be engaged to him in the first place. Any chance you want to come with me?"

I realized my mistake the moment the words left my lips. Shit. Shane wasn't the type of guy you brought to a wedding. He was intense and antisocial, for one thing. For another, we were merely having sex, not crossing all sorts of bridges into relationship land. "Sorry, forget I asked."

"Why? Don't want people knowing you're with the owner of a sex club?"

Not for the first time, I sensed some vulnerability around the subject, so I decided to put the topic to rest. "Honestly, I don't really care. Hell, I think half the people there would probably high-five me and the other half—Well, let's just say it's about time I stop caring about their opinion. After all, they thought Eric was a good guy, so what do they know?" I meant every word. My newfound resolution was to avoid trying to please others. From here on out, I was pleasing myself.

"Okay, I'll go."

"What?" I couldn't be more shocked. "Seriously?"

He shrugged. "Sure. Why not."

"You must really want butt sex."

He grinned. The expression, though rare, looked good on him. "You have no idea."

Chapter Sixteen

SHANE

"*W*hat the fuck was I thinking?" I said these words aloud to my best friend while getting ready to go pick up Daniella on Sunday afternoon. I couldn't believe I was going to a wedding—and with a date with whom I'd supposedly established boundaries.

"Beats me. You gonna try to catch the garter?"

Leave it to Max to fuck with me.

"Ha. And no. Maybe I should tell her I've changed my mind."

His eyes narrowed. "Dude. The girl calls and gets a plus one, thus able to save face in front of her ex by bringing a new date—and you want to bail? Even for you, that would be shitty."

I scrunched my face. "What the hell does *even for me* mean?"

"It means you aren't exactly into social graces. But if you'd wanted to back out, then fifteen minutes before you go pick her up is not the time. Man up. She's not like Tina, so I don't think you need to worry about her taking tonight the wrong way."

I hated it when he knew exactly what I was thinking. Then

again, I often returned the favor. "You're right. Unless you think you'll need help tonight?"

He shook his head. "New Year's Eve is the day after tomorrow. That's the party. Tonight will be the same old shit with the same old people. You should go and enjoy a rare Sunday evening off."

Rare was right. Seldom did I take a night completely off. If I did, it was typically a weekday, not on the weekend when things were busy. But I did plan on enjoying tonight. Hell, just the thought of having Daniella's ass made me hard. We'd been moving up the size of her plugs. I wasn't an anal virgin, but knowing she was had me all sorts of giddy.

Yes. Giddy. Like a fucking teenager.

Damn. I couldn't explain this hold she had over me, but the fact that even my dick had fallen suit was really getting to me. "Daniella indicated she should be done with the audit by Wednesday."

"So she said. In fact, I need to help her on Monday or Tuesday to reconcile some of the bar receipts. Heather is being less than obliging."

"Yeah. She's jealous of the attention I'm giving Daniella." I closed down the computer screen I'd been looking at and stood up. I was already dressed in a charcoal gray suit with a proper white, starched shirt and a blue tie. "Call me if you have any trouble."

Max laughed. "Sorry, buddy. No lifelines for you tonight."

ANY RESERVATION I had about attending a wedding quickly went out the window once Daniella opened her hotel room door. She was wearing a black strapless dress and her hair piled on top of her head in a curled coif.

"You look, uh, nice."

She rolled her saucy blue eyes. "Your compliments outside of the bedroom need work."

I watched while she grabbed her clutch and a small duffel bag. "Is that all you're bringing?"

She quirked her head to the side. "I don't plan on wearing a whole lot once I get out of this dress tonight."

I smiled, stepping closer so I could breathe in her scent. As I dropped a kiss to the curve of her neck, I loved how her breath caught at the simple action. "Lucky me, then. You look sexy."

Because my thoughts were turning carnal in a hurry, I retreated and offered my arm. We'd best go before I got the notion to fuck her on every available surface in her hotel room.

DANIELLA'S SMILE grew big when she spotted my Viper. What can I say? I loved a beautiful sports car. Of course it was black because that was my signature color. Maybe I liked things to match the color of my soul.

She slipped into the passenger seat after I held the door open for her, allowing me a tempting view of her toned legs. As soon as I was behind the wheel and started the car, I glanced over.

"Are you wearing panties?"

She smirked. "Only one way to find out."

I didn't hesitate to reach over. When my fingers met no barrier, coming into contact with her hot, wet heat, I smiled. Since she wasn't the type of girl who'd normally go commando, knowing she did it for me was even more of a turn-on.

I withdrew my hand, much to her frustration. But my options were limited while driving a stick shift. Plus it wasn't a long drive over to Jersey City.

Daniella blew out a breath, but then was distracted by her buzzing phone, which she answered. "Hey, Mom. No, we're on the way. We're not late. We're on time. Okay, fine. See you at the church."

She shut the phone with a big sigh. "I already can't wait to get to the reception and leave early."

I fought down the panic starting to well up. "Your mother is going to be there?"

She flipped down the visor and touched up her lipstick, either choosing to ignore the anxiety in my question or not recognizing it. "Yeah. Both her and my dad."

"You didn't mention that." Did she?

She flipped up the visor and capped her lipstick before glancing over. "I said it was for my cousin. I think that implies my family would be there."

"I don't do family." It was too much.

"What does that mean exactly?"

"It means I don't appreciate the blindside. I told you from the beginning this isn't a relationship."

Instead of looking upset, like I thought she would, she laughed. "I asked you if you wanted to come to my cousin's wedding. You said yes. Implying I sprang my family on you is complete crap. But you know what? Drop me off at the church. You're off the hook. The last thing I need is you thinking I somehow snared you into tonight."

Fuck. The guilt was already sinking in. "Look, it's nothing—"

She held up her hand. "Not trying to be rude here, but you don't owe me an explanation. I should've known better than to ask."

She was pissed, and I didn't blame her. It should've clicked when she'd said 'cousin's wedding' that it would include her family. But something didn't make sense. "Why would Eric be attending if it's your cousin's wedding?"

"Because the groom was his college roommate. They met at a happy hour for his firm that I dragged her to."

"Maybe I can go for a moment. That way Eric sees us and then—"

"Un—fucking—believable. I didn't invite you so I could save face. Whether I walk in there with you or by myself, my head is high. First, I did nothing wrong. Second, I don't care if he thinks I'm with someone or not."

Huh. Proving yet again that Daniella wasn't like most of the other women I knew. Any of them would've wanted to make their ex jealous. "I didn't mean to make it sound that way."

She was looking out the window, and I wasn't sure what else to say. Ten minutes later she directed me to the front of the church. I'd barely come to a stop before she was out of the car and shutting my door. I had to lower the window to shout out to her.

"Am I meeting you at the hotel later?"

She stopped for a moment, turned, and walked back to the car with purpose. There, she leaned down to the open window. "You know, for a smart man, that was a really dumb question. Especially when I'm sure you already can guess the answer."

I was a dick. And I'd screwed up. Big time. Knowing this only fueled my anger. My character and crappy judgment was why a guy like me did not belong even in a simple sex arrangement, let alone a relationship. Our argument was clearly a sign. But no-showing to a wedding after she'd called to bring a plus one was shitty. And it wasn't as though Daniella had given me any sign she was becoming attached or clingy. But meeting her parents... They would certainly have expectations about me, especially when Daniella was coming off her engagement.

Shit. It took me five minutes to make up my mind about what I needed to do.

Chapter Seventeen

DANIELLA

I should've known better than to ask him. Although it was an asshole move on his part to freak out at the last minute, it served as a reminder. I'd stepped out of the box into which we'd put our whatever-the hell-you-would-call-it, temporary, monogamous, non-kissing thing. But I'd meant what I said. I wasn't bringing him to save face. On the other hand, I had wanted him to be there as an ally. Someone who would be on my side, a person who represented unapologetic choices.

As I walked into the church, I kept my head high and gazed straight ahead. The last thing I wanted to do was mingle with anyone I didn't have to. Namely, Eric or any of his friends. My mother had already told me we'd be in the fourth row on the left side. I smiled at the usher, took the program, and allowed him to escort me down.

My mother, with her olive skin and big brown eyes, looked up smiling. She quickly dropped the expression for a frown. I already knew what was coming.

"Where is this date you insisted on bringing?"

"Unfortunately, something came up at work."

I took my seat and smiled at my dad. He was a big man

with the trademark Italian accent. "Hi, Dad. Looking good from the trip."

They were both sporting a glow from the Caribbean sun. "Hi, honey. Nice to see you."

But my mom wasn't done. "What do you mean he had to work? What does he do?"

"He manages a club in Manhattan. Something came up."

"Your cousin paid one hundred fifty per person."

I smiled tightly. "I'll send her a check and an apology."

"I swear, with your luck in men, Daniella, you're never going to settle down."

"Maybe I don't want to." I could tell from the intake of her breath she hadn't expected my retort.

She'd always preached that unless you had a ring on your finger and bun in the oven, you were not doing your part for society as a woman. "I saw Eric here, and he didn't bring a date. I'm certain if you guys talked things out, you could salvage the relationship."

"As I told you on the phone, he not only cheated on me, but he also stole from me. Is that who you really want as part of the family?"

My father wasn't helping. "You said he's paying you back. As for the other, maybe he just needed to get it out of his system."

Who were these people? If ever I wondered why I'd stayed longer than I should've in the relationship with Eric, these were certainly the influences. It made me even more grateful I'd gotten out. At least I didn't have to go home with them tonight and be surrounded by their disappointment like I would've had to do in my youth. Then again, when I was younger, I actually had done everything I could in order to please them. It had never been enough.

"I'm not discussing this here." I was done trying to please them.

The ceremony was about to start, and I already had a

headache. I was quickly thinking perhaps Shane had been right to bail. The thought slammed home when Eric stepped into our pew, much to my mother's delight.

"Here, dear, I saved a place for you."

His smile made me want to flee. With him now sitting between my mother and me, I seriously contemplated it. Only the onset of the wedding music stopped me.

"How are you?" he whispered.

"Shh. It's starting."

THE MOMENT the bride and groom made it to the back of the church, I bolted. It was only four blocks to the hotel where the reception was being held. I hoofed it rather than spend a moment longer in Eric's company. God, he'd been staring at me as my cousin and her new husband had been saying their vows like I would turn to him and say, 'let's get married.' If anything, the ceremony only reaffirmed my decision never to settle again.

Upon arriving at the hotel, I realized I'd beaten most guests there. Probably because they were doing some pictures after the ceremony, and people were mingling. At least this gave me time to go check in. Only one problem. My duffle bag was in Shane's car.

Not that I had a lot in there, but the contents did include my makeup bag, toiletries, and a change of clothes for tomorrow. Now, I had nothing but my purse and the hotel-provided items I'd find in the room. I sighed, thinking this was bad luck until it got worse.

"Can we talk for a minute?" Eric's voice came from behind me.

I accepted my key from the hotel clerk and turned around. "I have nothing to say to you unless the words out of your mouth are 'here's the rest of your money.'"

He winced. "Please keep your voice down. Look, there's no way I can get the rest of the money in two weeks."

I walked towards the elevators, already done with this conversation. "Then you'd best sell your car, condo, or a kidney."

"Come on, Daniella. I was talking to your mom, and she agrees we'd still be good together."

I lifted a brow. "Now that you don't have the money, you want to get back together. Unbelievable."

"What? She said you were showing up with some date, and you didn't."

"Says who?"

Shane's husky words came from behind me, but before I could turn to see him, he'd put his arm around my waist, intimately pinning my back to his front. Considering we'd been in much the same position the last time Eric had seen us together, I blushed.

"He's your date?" Eric stammered.

I'd be lying if I said I didn't get a lot of satisfaction from the look on his face. "It would seem so."

"You heading up to the room before the reception?" Shane whispered in my ear.

"Yes." I turned and saw he was holding my duffle along with his. "Thanks for bringing my bag."

He smirked. "Not a problem. Shall we?"

I gave one last glance toward Eric as Shane ushered me to the elevator, but my date wasn't done.

"Money to Dani in two weeks, Eric. Don't make her wait for it."

In epic, usually-only-see-it-in-the-movies fashion, the doors closed after his words, making Eric's face turn bright red.

I had goosebumps from Shane's don't-fuck-with-me tone. But it wasn't enough to override my annoyance from earlier.

I took a step to the side, but he wasn't having it. Instead he pulled me close, dipping his face into the crook of my neck and kissing the top of my shoulder.

"I'm sorry."

I pulled back to look at his face, shocked those words had come from him.

"Don't look so astounded. I do manage those words every once in a while. I came back for the ceremony, but it had already started, so I stood in the back. Then you all but bolted, so I couldn't catch up with you until now. It was a dick move to back out."

"It was, but I should've been clearer about the family element. To tell you the truth, after five minutes talking with my mother, I really can't blame you. I don't know what I was thinking."

"Why were you sitting by Eric in the church?"

The elevator stopped on my floor, and he followed me out. "My mother seems to think I should let bygones be bygones and trade in his pedigree for my self-worth."

"She wants you married with kids in the burbs."

I smiled sadly. "More than she wants my happiness."

He turned me, pinning me up against our room door. "And what do you want, Daniella?"

His gaze was burning into mine, and I found the breath catching in my chest. It was as though I had no choice but to utter my next words. "To feel free from the burden of being responsible for everyone else's happiness. Instead, I'd like to be responsible for just my own for once."

He cupped my face, running his thumb over my bottom lip in an intimate gesture. For a suspended moment in time, I was convinced he would kiss me. It could have been my imagination, but in his eyes, I saw the indecision. Then it was gone.

"What do you want, Shane?"

"To taste you before we go back downstairs."

The old me would've argued we didn't have time and

worried about being late. The new me was already wet with anticipation.

But if I'd thought it would be as expected, I should've known better. Shane had other ideas. Once the hotel room door opened, he backed me into the first available surface, which happened to be the desk, and dove under my dress.

"Hold up the bottom so I can see your face when you come for me."

"Oh, Good Lord." At this rate, we wouldn't be late at all. I was about to combust simply from the vibration of his words against my cleft.

"You taste amazing." His finger entered me and curled up. "Ah, and so wet."

He sucked on my clit while his finger moved in a rhythm that had me climaxing in a matter of minutes. But when he reached back, he froze.

"I wanted to surprise you." I'd put in one of the jeweled butt plugs. Not only was it a delicious type of foreplay, anticipating when he'd have me there, but I knew it would turn him on.

"Jesus, Dani. I'm rock hard for you. And I can't wait to be deep inside your ass."

He tugged on the plug, sending a zing straight to my center.

"How about now?" I was desperate for it and not above begging.

He stood up, his lips an inch from mine and still glistening from my wetness.

I couldn't help myself; I kissed him, groaning at the taste of myself on his lips until he pulled away.

"Sorry." But I wasn't because, for a moment, he'd returned my kiss.

He smiled. "I don't believe you. But because you're a naughty girl, you'll have to wait for me to have your ass. Now get on your knees and put your lips to good use."

It was the humor reflected in his eyes and the fact I was turned on which had me ignoring his bossy tone. Instead, I hopped down and unbuckled him, marveling at how hard he was. He lay heavy in my hand while I licked him from tip to base and enjoyed the way he sucked in his breath with the action.

Because I wanted to take him completely off guard, I swallowed him to the back of my throat in one motion, pulling back only to use my tongue to lubricate him and also my pinky finger.

"Jesus."

Music to my ears. I set a rhythm, bobbing on his cock like it was my mission in life to make him come as quickly as possible. And because I wasn't done with surprises and was curious about how Shane would react, I moved my pinky back and penetrated his backside with the coated little finger.

"Mother fucking—fuck."

He jerked his hips but then relaxed, allowing me to move it in further before he came spectacularly in my mouth.

SHANE

To say Daniella had just rocked my world was an understatement. She'd fucking annihilated it.

"Where did that trick come from?"

We'd finished cleaning up in the bathroom, where she was now reapplying her lipstick.

She shrugged. "I figured someone should at least get some ass play before we return for the reception."

I chuckled, loving her wit.

"I've never done it before. Did you like it?"

Although I wasn't normally into having my ass played with, her innocence and fearless way of trying new things was the biggest turn-on. I stepped into her, dropping my lips to her ear and grabbing her ass with both hands. "You have no idea. Now let's get downstairs before I fuck you on this vanity. Because you really don't know what you've started."

The slow, satisfied smile on her face let me know she was sorely tempted to find out and skip the reception. But if I was to make up for earlier, then I needed to ensure I escorted her downstairs.

By the time we walked into the ballroom, most people were seated and eating dinner. I hadn't been to many weddings in my lifetime, but it was clear, from the flowers to the china, that no expense had been spared on this one.

As we made our way towards our table, I swallowed hard, fighting the panic about meeting her parents. But she gave me a reprieve by leading us to the bar first.

"Figured you might want a whiskey first."

"You figured right. Uh, I—" I decided just to put the disclaimer out there while we were alone. "Look, I don't want to cause you any judgment from these people."

She straightened my tie, giving me a smile. "Let them judge away. I'm through caring. And think of it this way. You'll never have to see any of them again after tonight."

Right. The thought should've comforted me. But instead, for reasons I didn't want to examine, it annoyed me.

After we gathered our drinks and me my nerve, we made our way over to the table. A woman who had to be Daniella's mother sat beside a man who had to be her father.

The urge to flee was strong, but not as strong as my feelings for the woman beside me. Shit. Where had that thought come from? But I didn't have the time to examine it because introductions were happening.

I smiled tightly, taking my seat next to Daniella after I'd pulled out hers like a gentleman. The entire table went around introducing themselves: her aunt, uncle, a couple cousins and, last but not least, her parents.

"Why are you so late? And why did you take off after the

ceremony? We were looking for you for family pictures," her mother started in.

My annoyance immediately flared, but I noticed my date simply took a sip of her martini and replied, her lips twitching. "I found out Shane was able to make it and was waiting at the hotel."

"Yes, well, at least it's not wasted money with an empty place setting."

I gritted my teeth, thinking it was no wonder Daniella wanted company if this was her family.

She turned and gave me an apologetic smile.

We ate quickly, but not quickly enough. Her father leveled his eyes to mine. "So, Shane, what is it you do?"

I dabbed my mouth with my napkin. "I own a bar in Manhattan."

"What kind of bar?"

Before the wedding, I would have answered that question with the blunt truth. Absolutely, no question about it. But I couldn't do that to Daniella. I didn't want the disapproval at the table to be directed in the slightest towards her. "It's geared towards singles and requires a club membership."

Daniella about choked on her drink, obviously not expecting me to lie.

"Is it successful?" her mother asked.

"Mother, really?" Dani gave her a glare.

I waved a hand, used to this sort of interrogation from people. Although I was tempted to blurt out something equally tacky, like: *does clearing forty million over the last decade satisfy you*? But I managed not to. "Depends on your perspective. We've been in business ten years and operated in the black for nine. Matter of fact, I met your daughter when she started doing our taxes."

They got to stew on that tidbit while the toasts were made and the first dance started. When the other couples were invited out, I took Daniella's hand. "May I have this dance?"

She smirked and let me lead her out to the floor.

"What's with the smug look?"

"I was thinking you must really want anal tonight to put up with this and then ask me to dance."

I laughed, moving my hands down to inappropriately cop a feel on the subject matter. "I have no issue with dancing, and your mother's questions aren't unlike other judgments I've received over the last decade. And to think, she's made all these negative conclusions without even knowing it's a sex club."

She leaned back, studying my eyes. I swore she could see through all my defenses. "Did your mom judge you?"

"Yeah." But I didn't want to get into it here. "So back to the anal. When do you think we can get out of here?"

She leaned in, tightening her arms around me. "Mm. Maybe after a couple of dances. I'm kind of enjoying this. You look very handsome, by the way."

I was thankful she'd dropped the subject. "You look sexy, too, but I can't wait to see you in nothing but your plug."

We waited until the cake was cut, allowing Daniella to speak with her cousin, the bride, and get a couple photos before we went upstairs, drinks in hand. Neither of us had seen any sign of Eric at the reception. Most likely, he'd gone home. Just as well. I wasn't sure my capacity for civil behavior would hold out if he'd come around again.

As we entered the room, we laughed about how her great-aunt Mary had patted my ass after one too many cocktails.

I sipped my whiskey, watching while she slipped out of her heels and let her hair down. "You're beautiful." The words slipped out easily because it's what this woman was. Effortless beauty and class.

"Thank you. And thanks for coming back. I'm sorry my mom was so unpleasant."

I framed her face. "Don't ever apologize for someone else's actions, Dani. She is who she is."

She blew out a breath. "You're right. And I'm becoming less tolerant of it. Do you know, when I was little, I convinced myself that if I wasn't the perfect little girl, they'd send me back to where they'd adopted me?"

The thought made my stomach roll. "They said that to you?"

She shook her head. "No, no. But it's how I felt. Like they'd adopted me, and therefore I needed to be the daughter they wanted. Almost like I was obligated. But I don't feel that anymore. Instead, I feel like I'm done being that person."

"I'm a big fan of the way you are." I untied my tie and undid two of the shirt buttons. The vibe immediately changed. "Strip for me?"

She looked unsure for half a second, but then gave me one of her saucy smiles.

After slipping off my shoes, I got comfortable on the bed with the pillows behind my head at the top so I could watch. What I did in the club was normally rushed to the point where sex occurred. I didn't mind it because that was the ulti-mate goal. However, right now I wanted to savor. I wanted to appreciate. And then I wanted her ass.

DANIELLA

I unzipped my dress, trying to keep from being nervous. Wasn't as though this man hadn't already seen me naked. Besides, baring my innermost thoughts to him made me more vulnerable than the physical. But doing this deliberately was a little disconcerting. Especially with him watching me like a predator eyes its prey. Yet his frank appraisal brought me confidence. Somehow, I already knew tonight would be epic. Of course, that would only make it that much harder to think about leaving in three days' time. But for now, well, I was seizing the moment.

Once I was down to merely my lacy bra, his husky voice broke me out of my thoughts. "Turn around. And after you lose the bra, bend over and let me see that plug."

Damn. I'd started this game, however, and I was determined to give him the show he craved.

I could hear his muttered curse when I did what he asked, but was unprepared for his next request.

"Come here and sit on my face."

Huh. I'd kind of thought we'd get right to it, but clearly he had other plans. Never having assumed this position, I wasn't sure how to accomplish it. But he took control once I approached the bed, lifting me up by the waist and having me straddle his shoulders.

"Grab the headboard for leverage."

"Oh, fuck."

He hadn't hesitated, instead devouring me from this angle, pressing my pussy into his face by gripping my ass. "Ride it like you want it, baby."

I was digging the term of endearment, but not as much as the newfound sensation of him having all access. One of his fingers was pushing the plug while others were up inside of me, working together with his mouth to have me exploding on his face in no time. But he wasn't done. Instead, he replaced his fingers with his tongue.

"Ohhhhhhh." I was pretty sure my words were only a jumble as my eyes rolled back, and all that was present was white light in the climax which washed over me.

I didn't know how he managed it, but the next thing I registered was being on my back. I opened my eyes to see him shedding his clothing in record time and then rolling on the condom. He was between my thighs and thrusting deep inside of me before my aftershocks had stopped.

"Christ, I love it when your cunt grips me, and I can still feel your orgasm."

My nails raked down his back, and I reveled in the feel of his skin.

Suddenly, he pulled out. "Get on your knees, gorgeous."

As I did so, he crossed the room and came back with a bag in hand.

"What's that?"

"Toys. Now be a good girl and put those pillows under your stomach to help support you."

I could hear the sound of lube before I felt him take the plug out. He replaced it with his readied fingers. "You're fucking perfect. And because I want to give you ultimate pleasure, I'm putting this in your pussy."

I gasped at the sensation of the large dildo being placed inside of me and then moaned when it started to vibrate.

"This is only the head of my cock. To work you in. We'll go slow."

I burned a little despite being readied, and I was even more thankful he'd been courteous enough to work me in over the last two days. I appreciated that he was talking me through it.

"Just an inch. That's it. Relax and let me in."

I sucked in my breath as he made it past the ring of muscle, deeper inside of me.

"Christ, your ass is tight. I can't wait to bottom out in you, Daniella, and fuck you hard. You want that, don't you?" He slipped in another inch.

"Yes. Oh, God." I was quickly becoming overwhelmed by what was happening to my body. My legs were shaking while my desire was at a precipice it had never been. If his stuttered breaths were any indication, Shane was having a hard time with control.

"I'm almost there. You okay?"

"Uh-huh. Shane, I—" Whatever I'd been thinking to say evaporated. Rooted, he'd started moving while working the dildo in tandem. It was as though all my brain synapses exploded in the tidal wave of the climax washing over me. My body was on autopilot, bucking against his thrusts and seemingly going from one orgasm into another. As I was about to black out, I heard him grunt his own climax with a string of curses following. Then it went black.

SHANE

Making a woman come like Daniella had should be the crowning achievement of manhood. I washed her intimately, smiling as she hardly moved, merely murmuring a thanks and something about being boneless. Then I put the blanket up around her, unsure what to do next.

I didn't spend the night with a woman. Ever. Yet the last thing I wanted to do was ditch her to find her own way back to New York in the morning, especially after my epic screwup earlier. Fuck. I really hadn't thought this whole hotel night thing out. So I took a long hot shower. Then I slipped into the bed, naked and already hard again. I'd decided to take care of things myself when she shocked me by speaking.

"You're not wasting a hard-on with me in the bed naked next to you?"

I froze mid-stroke. "You were kind of passed out."

"I needed a few minutes. You pretty much rocked my world."

She scooted over to me, and I tensed. I was not accustomed to naked cuddling or the skin on skin contact. Hell, it would be too easy to slide right into her about now. And her kisses down my neck were doing nothing to halt the temptation to do just that. I was on the brink of sinking into her heat without anything between us.

"Did the test results come back clean?" I couldn't believe I was asking this question. I'd never been bareback with any woman.

"Yes."

"I can show you my test results."

"I'm not on the pill."

"I got a vasectomy, so I won't get you pregnant."

She popped up, her expression full of surprise. I wondered if I'd managed to slam shut any hope she might have about a future with me. I told myself it was for the best. But instead, she smiled.

"Good, because I don't want children."

I hardly had time to analyze her statement before she hit me with her next words. "But don't you think it would be odd to go bare and not kiss?"

She was right. And I was crazy to have suggested it. "You're right. It was a stupid thought. Hold tight." I jumped out of bed and retrieved a condom, putting it on in record time while avoiding her eyes. I didn't want to see the disappointment that I'd been about to fuck her bare but didn't want the intimacy of a kiss.

"Shane, are you upset?"

I plastered a smile on my face and forced myself to lose the tension. "Only at myself for losing my head for a moment. Now spread those legs and let me in."

Chapter Eighteen

DANIELLA

*T*he man had fucked me into a coma. That's why, when the light came on and Shane's voice woke me, I could hardly manage an acknowledgement.

"Come on, sleepyhead. I need to get back."

I ran my hands over my face and winced at the soreness all over my body. "Do I have time for a shower?" I definitely needed one, not only to clean up, but also to get my wits about me.

"Just enough if you get up now."

I opened my eyes slowly and realized he was already dressed, looking ready to go. I slid naked from the bed, not missing the appreciation in his expression when I did so.

"You want to join me?"

"Can't. I, uh, have a call. Be quick, and I'll get the car brought around."

Well, if that wasn't a dismissal, I didn't know what was. Sighing, I realized something had changed since last night. He'd retreated. Maybe it was the line he had suggested we cross last night by using no protection. Or maybe he wasn't comfortable waking up with a woman. For whatever reason, he was definitely acting strange.

When I got into the car fifteen minutes later, he occupied himself with anything but conversing with me.

"Everything okay?" I refused to sit there getting the silent treatment.

"Yeah, fine. But tomorrow is New Year's Eve, the busiest night of the year."

"Oh. I didn't realize. Anything I can help with?"

"Nope. Matter of fact, if you want to take off today, I'm sure things can wait."

In other words, he didn't want me around. "I'd prefer to get some things done today so I can possibly finish up by tomorrow."

"Suit yourself."

Evidently, I would.

I WORKED until four o'clock that afternoon, frustrated that Heather's bar receipts weren't adding up. Either she was keeping some stuff from me in order to torture me or make me look inept, or she was hiding something. I rubbed my temples, wondering if I should leave this to fresh eyes in the morning.

That's when Max came up. "Hey, you planning to attend the New Year's Eve party tomorrow night?"

"Uh, I'm not sure. What does it entail?"

He chuckled. "Not a gang bang. At least, not including you. It'll be like the Christmas party, only more festive because of the countdown. Make sure you stick to the main floor, though. Don't go into the basement."

"There's a basement?"

"No. No. And no," came Shane's words from the elevator doors, which had just opened to reveal him.

"There isn't a basement?" I played coy, enjoying that it

instantly irritated him. Considering he'd ignored me all day, I wasn't sorry.

"There is, but you're not going to the main floor, let alone the basement, which Max shouldn't have mentioned to you. I'll have enough on my mind without worrying about you in that crowd."

"Yes, well, I'm not your responsibility, Shane."

"You're working here, so yes, you are."

I turned towards Max, who was looking amused at our exchange. "You know, I'll have to see how this job goes with my pain-in-the-ass, temporary boss. Suddenly, I have the urge to work longer hours to get this assignment done." I gathered the rest of my stuff and turned off the desk lamp. "Good night, gentleman."

As I lay in my bed later that night waiting for the knock which never came, I realized I needed to heed my own words. It was time to be done with whatever I'd had with Shane. Although I'd told myself it was only sex, my wounded feelings were calling me a liar.

SHANE

If we'd been in a relationship, which we weren't, I would have chased after her. Knocked on her door and fucked her into understanding I didn't want her around the sometimes rowdy crowd that attended New Year's Eve. But we weren't, which is why I was nursing my whiskey, hard and alone, in my condo a couple blocks away. I looked out the windows over the city and tried not to wonder what Daniella would think of the view. Then I cursed myself for the thought. I realized the best thing for both of us would be for her to finish the job and move on.

The next morning I was at the club at the crack of dawn. I

loved this hour because there weren't a lot of people about. The chef, a couple security guys, but no patrons since we didn't open the doors until three o'clock. Even then, it never got busy before nine.

After I climbed the stairs to my office, I was shocked to see Daniella already at my desk, poring over receipts and typing into her spreadsheet. I took a moment, drinking her in, hating that after one night without her, I'd missed her.

"Good morning."

She looked up but didn't smile. "'Morning."

"You're here early."

"I was hoping a fresh start would help fill in the holes in the information Heather provided me. It hasn't."

I sighed, thinking Heather would go ballistic if Daniella questioned her. "What's missing?"

She frowned. "I don't know."

I walked towards her and looked over her shoulder at a spreadsheet that would make my eyes cross. "If you don't know, then how can you accuse—?"

"Whoa, I'm not accusing. I'm simply stating that something doesn't add up. Considering she wasn't exactly forthcoming with all of the requested information, it could be a matter of that, or it could be my lack of understanding. Maybe I need a tutorial on the inventory."

"Aside from Heather, Max is the most familiar with the bar area. I'm sure when he comes in, he can give you one."

I wasn't trying to blow her off. It was just fact. Max loved to man the bar from time to time as his roots were in bartending. My expertise was more on the financials and security. But Daniella's face betrayed she wasn't buying it.

"Okay, I'll speak to Max, then."

"Look, it isn't personal. He really does know the bar better than I do."

She took off her glasses and leveled me with her gaze.

"Some of the girls mentioned you normally perform on New Year's Eve. If you want out of our agreement for that, then I'd understand."

Would she, now? The thought instantly pissed me off. "Oh, yeah? You're okay with the thought of me fucking another woman?"

She flinched, and I knew I'd gone too far. "Maybe I wouldn't care."

My brows went high. If it weren't for her blush or the fact she couldn't meet my gaze, I might've believed her. I pulled her up for her chair, and framed her face with my hands. "You wouldn't care, huh?"

She lifted her chin while defiance showed in her eyes.

"You wouldn't care if it's not your mouth on me, not your pussy or your ass that I'm fucking?" I was pushing her, recognizing the last thing I wanted was for her not to care. Because the very thought of her with another man made me feel like I was going to lose my shit. Which is one of the reasons I didn't want her down on the floor. It was also why I was trying, unsuccessfully, to wean myself off of her.

"I wouldn't want to," she finally relented, maybe not expecting the same feelings I was warring with.

"Me, either. Come on." I led her into the bedroom next door and quickly lost my jacket and tie.

"What are you doing?"

"What I should've been doing last night. Fucking you senseless."

"The wedding and morning after freaked you out, didn't it?"

Clearly, she needed an explanation before anything would happen. Not exactly the order I would've preferred, but I got it. "Yes. I didn't know what to do. That isn't my world, and this isn't yours. And this thing between us is more than I expected." There, I'd manned up and said it.

"For me, too. But there's something more. A reason you won't kiss me. A reason you freaked about family and then spending the night. What is it?"

I didn't want to get into this. But perhaps telling her would make her understand. "There was a girl I met when I was visiting my mom for the holidays about ten years ago. She was home from college. We went out twice. I'd just purchased the club and took her here for our second date when she'd indicated she wanted to have sex. We had fun. But then she developed feelings. I had to break it to her that I didn't feel the same. She accused me of leading her on. And hell, maybe I had."

"By doing what?"

"Kissing. Holding hands. Taking her on dates. It all screams relationship."

"Not after two times."

"That's what Max said. What's worse is she told my mother, about me owning a sex club."

She sucked in a breath. "Crap. What ended up happening?"

"My mom, who is very conservative and worried about everyone else's opinion told me to choose between the family or the club."

"And she never came around?"

"Not even on her deathbed. She didn't even want to see me. She died just as disappointed in me as she'd been the day I begged her not to make me choose. Since the fiasco with Tina, I've tried to be very clear about my intentions and that I don't want a relationship. And I've become unapologetic with those who judge me regarding the choices I've made."

She put her arms around me. "No wonder a wedding with family freaked you out. Your mother never should've made you choose. But as for my intentions, I mean what I say, Shane. This may be more than I bargained for, but I know what it is. And more importantly, what it isn't."

I'd expected to be relieved. But shockingly, I wasn't. "When you talked before about wanting to feel free, Daniella, I know what you're craving." What I didn't say was that sometimes there was a cost to it all. Disappointment in those you love didn't come cheap.

Her hand stroked my face. And now it was time to get back to even ground.

"Turn around. Face the wall and put your hands up to brace yourself. We don't have much time, so I'm going to fuck you fast. Then this afternoon before things get busy, I'm taking you into one of the rooms downstairs before it gets busy. And we're playing."

She swallowed hard before turning around to put her hands on the wall and then spreading her feet.

I grabbed her ass, enjoying how her burgundy fitted dress hugged her curves, matched her hair, and showed off her assets. Assets that, for the time being, were all mine to do with as I pleased.

I ran my hand up the inside of her thighs and came into contact with her thong. "Tsk, tsk, you didn't follow instructions, Daniella." My hand smacked her backside with enough of a sting to make her squeal.

"Oh."

Rubbing the area, I whispered in her ear. "Did you enjoy that?"

She pushed her ass back toward my ever-growing erection. "I didn't think I would, but I like it when you do it."

"God, how I wish I had more time. Later, we'll play."

I found the foil packet in my wallet and slipped the condom on, afterward wasting no time sinking into her heat and thrusting up. Reaching around, I strummed her clit and enjoyed how quickly I could make her come. I was quick to follow, grinding out my orgasm deep inside of her while my hands tangled with hers against the wall.

Stepping back, I quickly tied off the condom and tucked

myself back into my pants. "I'll see you at three o'clock. Room forty-two."

Chapter Nineteen

DANIELLA

$\mathcal{A}$fter my quickie with Shane, I went over the bar inventory with Max, trying to focus even though I was distracted by the events of the morning.

I'd wanted to argue with Shane when he'd said that was my world and this was his. Tell him we could possibly find some sort of middle ground. But then I realized I'd be going against everything I'd agreed to. At least he'd acknowledged this was more intense than either of us could've guessed it would be. And he'd confided in me about where his trust issues came from. But all the information did was confirm the fact he'd never had or ever wanted a relationship. I knew from experience that monogamy could never compete with what he had here at the club.

All of this told me I was better off recognizing this was ending on Wednesday. But if I was to make that happen, I needed to understand what Max was telling me.

"So the liquor arrives from the distributor in boxes?"

He nodded. "Yes. Normally in four, six, or ten packs."

"And how can I tell what arrives in what?"

He frowned. "It should tell you on each packing slip."

I held one out for him.

He looked perplexed after scanning it. "Weird. There's a total, and the box number, but not how many units per package."

"Exactly. That's my problem. From the prices, I can determine they weren't singles, but unless I know the count, I can't figure out if they're correct."

"We should be able to get you the boxes. I don't get why the number of units aren't printed on there. I seem to remember seeing they were in the past. But maybe since Heather knows the counts, she hasn't questioned it."

Or maybe she was stealing. I didn't want to believe it simply because Max and Shane would be devastated, but things weren't adding up. Literally.

"When does the next inventory come in?"

"Later this afternoon in prep for the party. I'm sure Heather could—"

I was already shaking my head. "That's not gonna work." Heather was not about to do me any favors, and I was now very suspicious of her.

He chuckled. "Yeah, she's pretty pissy since finding out about you and Shane."

"Why, though? In a couple days it'll be over, and I'll be gone."

He quirked his head to the side. "Is that what you want?"

He appeared sincere in his question, and for a moment I thought about being truthful. But this was Shane's best friend. I chose to stay neutral and not reveal too much. "It's what we agreed to."

"Agreements can be amended."

One of the guys stepped in, calling for Max.

"It's okay. I know you're busy. But later this afternoon after the order comes in, can you show me what a typical one looks like? It'll only take a few minutes."

"Uh, sure. But I'll have to figure out something to tell

Heather. Inventory is kind of her baby, and she gets territorial over it."

I bet.

I WALKED into room forty-two right on time and found Shane waiting in a high wingback chair. Unlike the last time I'd been in one of these rooms, I wasn't nervous. Instead, I was full of delicious anticipation for what he had in store.

Smiling, I walked towards him, my gaze on his.

"Stop there and strip."

Whereas this morning had been quick and hurried, I could tell he would now take his time. I started with my boots and then shimmied out of my thong. After that, I removed my stockings and, finally, my dress and bra.

He leaned forward, eyes simmering with lust. "I've been fantasizing about something since the first time I met you."

I swallowed hard. "What's that?"

"You touching yourself in front me. Making yourself come."

My sigh was audible. "I've never—"

But he wasn't having it. "You've never had me talking you through it. Try. For me?"

How could I possibly say no?

"Take a seat on this chair and spread your legs."

I did as he requested, watching in stunned silence when he knelt in front of me and put his hands on my thighs.

"I want to be up close and personal while I watch you. Spread your lips; show me that pretty pussy."

My fingers from one hand dipped down and spread myself open. I was very aware of how close he was. The fingers from my other hand found my clit and rubbed circles.

"Damn, that's sexy. Do you have any idea how much I want to dive in and taste you? How I plan to put you on the bed and pleasure you with toys and my cock? I'm going to fuck you in your mouth first. I have dreams about how well you suck me off. Then I'm putting a long dildo in your ass while I fuck your pussy at the same time. And finally, I'm going to come all over your luscious body. Mark you with it."

"Oh, Jesus." I was rubbing faster and faster with his dirty words, wanting all of it and more.

"That's it, Dani. Make yourself come, and I'll lick up your mess."

"Fuck." I was there. I was coming under my own hand. I let my head fall back as the climax washed over me. But before I could come down from the rush, Shane was there, pulling my hips into his face and eating me with such abandon it seemed like mere seconds before I was coming again, calling out his name.

"That was the hottest thing I've ever seen." His face was still shiny with my wetness as he traveled up to suck on my nipple, giving it a tug with his teeth before doing the same with the other one. "Stay here."

As I watched with appreciation while he stripped out of his clothes, I found my hand making it's way back between my legs. I was so very hot for him.

"Christ. I can hear how wet you are. Use this. Make yourself come again."

He produced a dildo from a package, handing it over already vibrating. I inserted it, letting my eyes flutter closed with the sensation. But they snapped open when he pulled me onto the edge and put my feet on a stool, allowing me to be completely bared for him. I felt a pressure at my backside and realized he was pushing something hard and lubricated inside. I sucked in a shuddered breath at the sensation.

"You have no idea how sexy you are. Play with yourself and come again while I have your mouth."

He positioned himself at my head, feeding me his cock one glorious inch at a time. I was anxious for the taste of him, but finding it hard to concentrate as I didn't have the use of my hands. "Allow me."

He took over for the dildo, pumping it deep inside me while I took a hold of his length and went to work.

"Come with me, baby. I want to feel it while you swallow it down."

My body erupted, and as a result, his did too. Although an orgasm made it tough to remember to swallow, I managed to get most of it in my mouth. The rest spilled onto my chest, which served to turn him on even more.

"Christ, I love the sight of my cum on your tits. But I'm not done with you."

I was grateful when he scooped me up and lay me on the bed because I wasn't sure I had the strength to do it under my own power. I'd lost the vibrator, but he'd kept the dildo in my ass. He was now moving that slowly.

"Are you sore?"

"A little, but not bad."

"Good."

He quickly put on a condom and was on top of me in minutes. "Wrap your legs around me, gorgeous, and hold on. I'm going to pound you hard."

Although I'd just had three intense orgasms, my body was greedy for more. So when he entered me, I tightened my intimate muscles around him, liking the way I'd taken him off guard.

"Jesus."

The only thing missing, however, was the way he buried his face in my neck instead of taking my lips. But I didn't have time to dwell on the disappointment because he was giving me another orgasm, followed by flipping me over and taking me hard from behind. The primal sound of flesh smacking flesh filled the room. He insisted on another and then another, stealing them from my body as if in a challenge.

Then he did as he'd promised, losing the condom and coming all over my ass.

"Let's take a shower, and then I need to get prepared for the party."

Right. The party. Where did this man get his energy?

Chapter Twenty

DANIELLA

*N*ew York City was absolutely nuts for New Year's Eve, which is why I'd spent most of my life avoiding the place on that night. But tonight I was in the absolute heart of it, in a sex club, of all places. Ironically, I was doing the books, the most nonsexual activity possible.

Since it was the bar that was giving me trouble, I went down to the stock room, hoping to see the newly delivered boxes in order to get my brain wrapped around what was missing.

"What? Are you checking up on me now?" Heather appeared in the doorway.

"I'm doing an audit, which means I'm checking up on everything, not everyone."

"Look, just because I fucked Shane before you got here and certainly will fuck him again after you leave, doesn't give you the right to single me out."

"That's absurd. I'm simply trying to understand the invoices so I can make sense of them."

"Then why are you down here? Shouldn't you be at your computer if it's a matter of you not understanding the invoices?"

I bristled at her tone but kept my face neutral. "Actually, I'm meeting Max."

He came into the stock room, obviously having received my text message that I was ready to meet. He looked from me to Heather. "Hey, ladies. Uh, where is the delivery?"

"I already unloaded everything. What, now you're in on this investigation, too, Max?"

I found it an interesting choice of words but stood quiet.

He sighed. "Look, I don't have time for this. She's doing a job, Heather. That's all. And sorry, Daniella. At the next delivery, I'll walk you through the process."

Heather bristled. "The hell you will. And the next delivery isn't until Wednesday. Shane indicated she'd be gone by then. After all, he has his scheduled performance on Friday night."

A slap in the face would've felt better. The satisfied look on Heather's face told me she knew it.

I watched her walk out and gave a fake smile to Max. Then something occurred to me. "Where would the emptied boxes be taken?"

"There's a dumpster out back. They should be there. You want me to help you look?"

I shook my head, knowing he and Shane were insanely busy trying to get things ready. "No, no. I'm fine on my own. Thanks."

I purposefully made a show out of going up the front stairs back to the office so Heather would see me. Then I grabbed my winter coat, because it was absolutely freezing outside, and went down the back stairs. I wasn't surprised that I didn't find any of the boxes in the two dumpsters. What in the hell was she hiding? I couldn't explain my determination except that I was certain I was onto something.

After stomping back up to the office, I found Shane at my desk.

"Hey, where were you?"

"Trying to get a sense of inventory, but Heather had already unloaded and stocked up."

He didn't seem bothered by it. "It's a busy night. She probably did it early to get ahead."

"The next delivery isn't until Wednesday morning."

I didn't miss the way his shoulders tensed. "Is it that important? If you're still struggling with the inventory numbers and don't want to talk to Heather about it, then write down your questions for me or for Max. We'll try to get you the answers."

In other words, he didn't want me staying. In other words, he thought the problem was my lack of understanding. And of course, there was the performance he was already moving on to once I left. "Right. Well, I guess I'll figure out what I can. Um, how many boxes do you get during a normal delivery, by the way?"

"Not sure. Sometimes a hundred or so. I'm sure today's was extra large. We get deliveries twice a week. I've gotta go, but I'll, um, talk to you later, okay?"

I nodded. Then I realized I wanted to go back outside. A hundred boxes couldn't have gone far. And maybe I had something to prove to Shane: that my hunch wasn't unfounded.

AN HOUR LATER, my fingers were absolutely frozen. I'd tromped around to all the businesses in the area, looking inside of their dumpsters. I had nothing to show for it. Since neither the recycling nor trash trucks had come through on New Year's Eve to empty the dumpsters, Heather had to be hiding something.

"Where the hell have you been?"

Shane looked like he'd been waiting for me when I

returned to the office, but I didn't appreciate his tone. "I went outside and walked around a bit."

He stepped closer, taking my hands in his to warm them. "Jesus. Without gloves? I told you I don't want to have to worry about you tonight. How about you go back to the hotel?"

"Why? What is this really about?"

He sighed. "I have a big shot coming in tonight who'll be using the viewing room up here. He does this every year. He's obnoxious, rich, and believes he can buy anything with money. If he sees you, he'll assume you're one of the girls here."

"So I tell him I'm not."

Shane shook his head. "He isn't someone you say no to. The last thing I want is to have to step in and piss him off. Even worse, I'd come unglued if I saw him paw at you."

I occurred to me that in a normal relationship, Shane would simply tell the guy I was with him. But this wasn't such a thing. Besides, it wasn't like we'd be kissing at midnight. "Sure, I can work from my room at the hotel. Will I see you later?"

"I'll be lucky if I'm out of here before four in the morning. But we have one last night tomorrow night. Okay?"

Yep. Emphasis on last. "Sure. I guess Happy New Year."

He smiled, already looking tired. "Yeah, Happy New Year."

As SOON AS I arrived at my hotel room, I went to work with my sleuthing skills. I needed to get box counts. If I could get a quote for the same types of liquor, it would give me an idea for the number of bottles in a box. So I called the distributor, but as I should have expected this late on New Year's Eve, I got no one. When I went to the website, I discovered I wouldn't be able to get anyone until the day after tomorrow.

Shit. I couldn't wait until Thursday. I'd be gone by then. I'd even made vacation plans to make sure I wouldn't wallow here after my last day. And although I had good computer skills, I wasn't advanced enough to hack into the distributor's client accounts. And, yes, I tried.

Frustrated, I was about to give up, but then I came up with an idea. Club Travesty couldn't be the only place around serviced by this distributor. However, the chances of anyone answering the phone this late were slim. Which meant I'd be going out for New Year's Eve.

My first stop was downstairs at the hotel bar, but I wasn't in luck. They used a smaller scale supplier than Club Travesty's. But they did tip me off that the sports bar around the corner most likely used the same distributor as the club. So, two blocks down, I went amongst the growing number of people and into the bar.

It was just my luck the place was packed. When I asked to see the manager, the snippy hostess appeared completely put out. Shit, maybe I should've waited until tomorrow.

When the large man, sporting tattoos on his rippling biceps, came to the front, looking none to happy to be bothered, I almost bolted. Only the adrenaline from the chase gave me the courage to stay put.

"What's the problem?"

"No problem. Um, I'm Daniella, and my client is currently using a distributor named Wicked Liquor. I was wondering if you use them?"

"Yeah, what of it?"

"Well, I'm doing the books and found the box counts are missing from my receipts. I wondered if Wicked Liquor is doing the same with other clients."

"Call them to ask."

Oh, boy. "I would, but it's New Year's Eve."

"No shit. This place is a zoo, and I have you asking me about suppliers on the busiest night of the year. What club are you at?"

"You're right, and I'm sorry. I'm with Club Travesty."

"You know Max?"

"Yes, Max and Shane."

"Why didn't you say so? What do you need?"

"Uh, just your last order. You can redact the amounts; I'm only interested in the box counts for each type of liquor."

"Sure. You want to come back with me to the office?"

Nope. Not even a little. "If you don't mind, I'll wait out here."

"No problem."

He was back in ten minutes with papers in his hands and an apologetic look on his face. "Uh, spoke with Shane. Hope you don't mind me verifying you're with the club. He said to give these to you, but he was pissed you were here. Told me to tell you to get your ass back to your hotel room."

I bristled. Not because the bar manager had called the club. I should've expected that. But because Shane was treating me as though I was under curfew. "Thanks for the paperwork, uh—Sorry, I didn't catch your name."

"Joe, and you're welcome. And you're not going back, are you?"

I smirked. "Nope. Suddenly I feel like a drink."

Chapter Twenty-One

SHANE

*A*fter hanging up the phone with Joe, I had one thought.

I was going to kill her. I'd asked for one simple thing. For Daniella to stay in her hotel room. But evidently, that was too much. And what the hell was she doing asking for Joe's inventory forms? It occurred to me that I could've told him not to give her the paperwork, but I was too curious about why she wanted it to do that.

As if the night wasn't already off to a busy start, I'd already had to have two people escorted out for being intoxicated and had been obliged to break up a cat fight. Added to that, Mr. Moneybags was in rare form, causing my staff to kiss his ass and that of his entourage. I had to remind myself he'd paid a hundred thousand dollars for the box suite and he tipped the girls, some of whom were quite happy to service him.

And now I had to go drag Daniella's ass back. Joe had called back to inform me she hadn't taken my advice and was now sitting at his bar. Fuck.

I walked in and noticed the place was packed, as were

most bars now that it was close to midnight. Yet she stood out with her copper hair down her back and a lyrical laugh at something Joe was saying to her from behind the bar.

I wasted no time stepping up and settling my hands at her waist.

She instantly tensed, but then must've realized it was me.

Joe gave me a nod. "What's up, Shane?"

"Busy night. You?"

"Same."

"You ready?" I whispered in her ear.

"Actually, no. I think this beats spending New Year's Eve by myself in my room."

"How many has she had?"

Joe chuckled. "Only one, my friend. I think perhaps you met your match."

"Indeed. Let's go, Dani." I used a tone which didn't leave room for argument, and yet she was able to ignore it.

She spun around. "And if I'm not ready to go?"

"Then I can get you ready." I let the implication settle and was relieved to see her smile.

"Well, then. In that case." She turned saying goodbye to the bar manager. "Nice to meet you, Joe."

I led her outside and down the sidewalk at breakneck speed, already hard at the thought of sneaking in a quickie with her before returning to the club. It was crazy to think this would be our third time today and yet I still hadn't had enough.

"I'm going to sit in your hotel chair where you'll ride me reverse cowgirl while I play with your ass. But after that, I need to get back to work."

"You don't have to do me any favors, you know. And you're not my keeper. I went to bars by myself before I met you. You don't get to tell me what to do."

I backed her up against the cold brick wall of the nearest

building and let her feel my erection through the layers of clothing between us. "Point taken. Now am I taking you to your hotel room or leaving you here?"

My phone interrupted. "What?" I answered tersely.

"Moneybags is asking for you. Where are you?" Max's voice came over.

"Shit. Give me two minutes." I hung up, looking at Daniella and already feeling regret. "I need to get back to work."

We both looked around when people started counting down. It only got louder as they got closer. "Five, four, three, two, one. Happy New Year."

Our eyes locked. I didn't miss the disappointment which flashed in hers when I pulled away, not even willing to give her a kiss when it hit midnight.

We walked in silence back to the hotel entrance where she gave me a small wave and went into the lobby.

For the first time, I felt torn between the club and a woman.

It WASN'T until four o'clock in the morning that we cleared every room. I was on my second Red Bull and Max had gone straight for black coffee. Even Heather was uncharacteristically quiet while she wiped down the bar and put the last few things away.

Housekeeping had started their impossible task of cleaning up every room, and my security detail was due to change over in another hour. In all, it had been a good party, but I was over the holiday season and all its festivities. Thankfully, we wouldn't have another one until summer. Tomorrow would be a fairly quiet day, and I looked forward to spending the night with Daniella. Knowing it would be our last night was leaving me restless. I reasoned it was because it was time to start getting back to normal. Put the holidays behind me and get back into the routine of things.

Speaking of which, I had a show on Friday night with a performer by the name of Donna Starr who'd be in town one night. I'd been with her before. She was spectacular at putting on a show, and I should be looking forward to it. The woman could suck a penny through a fifty-foot hose. Yet the thought of someone other than Daniella on her knees in front of me left me uninspired.

Crap. What was with this girl? Luckily, I had one more night to fuck her out of my system. Then she'd be back to her life, and I'd be back to mine. All I needed was some separation to get her off my mind.

I sent Max home to get some sleep while I prepared to make it an all-nighter. I'd catch a nap later if I got too tired.

DANIELLA

I brought coffee in for Max, Shane, and myself. They had to be even more exhausted than I was this morning. Knowing Shane, he probably hadn't slept at all.

I'd stayed up late looking at the delivery sheets from Joe's bar, attempting to match up the liquor types with quantities. Unfortunately, the amounts told a confusing story. It seemed Travesty was not getting the better deal. It might have made sense if Joe's bar had more inventory. Then it would be understandable they'd be getting a better discount than the club. But judging from the slips and what had arrived at the club earlier today, we should have been the ones getting the bigger discount. Furthermore, numbers weren't adding up. One case of Patron, for example, should contain four bottles. Yet it appeared we were being charged for ten. Same with the

Grey Goose. And that was just on the stuff we had in common with Joe's place. I knew for a fact that Travesty stocked some premium Scotch at four hundred dollars a bottle and some champagne worth the same. The sports bar wouldn't. By the time I was done estimating, I calculated an approximate discrepancy of between three to five thousand dollars per delivery. If I multiplied that times twice a week, it could be like sixty thousand a month, if not more. The numbers corresponded with the loss I'd been looking for, but unfortunately, I had no absolute proof. Just a hunch to dig further for it.

If I stayed for Thursday's order, that would provide the proof. And what was one more day, really? I was sure when I explained this to Shane and Max they'd be just as anxious as I to see if Heather was stealing.

I was right about Shane pulling an all-nighter. This was evident when he came up the stairs a few minutes after I'd arrived. "You look tired."

"I am. And you look like you've been busy."

I had paperwork spread out all over the desk, attempting to paint the picture I wanted to share with both him and Max. "I am. Here, I got you coffee. One for Max, too."

"He's catching a few hours but will be back soon. I'm sure he'll appreciate it."

"Everything okay from last night?"

"Yeah. Just busy. I'll be glad to get back to normal."

I had to bite my lip, wondering if part of the 'abnormal' had to do with me. "Definitely. Uh. So I think I've found your discrepancy, but I'd rather wait for Max to be here in order to discuss it."

"Did I hear my name?" A bleary-eyed Max came out the elevator doors.

I smiled and handed over a coffee. "You did. Here."

"You're a saint, Daniella. Thanks."

"Is, uh, Heather around?" The last thing I wanted to do was have this conversation if she could walk up or overhear it.

"Nope," Max remarked. "She's off today. Will be in Thursday morning, though. Why?"

"Well, actually, one of the things I wanted to talk to you about is coming in on Thursday for the delivery. I'd like for both of you to be there, too."

"Why?" Shane asked sharply.

"Because Thursday would show—"

"You said tomorrow was your last day. Whatever you have today is what we've got. And what does it have to do with Heather?"

I tried to fight the hurt that he didn't want me here even for one extra day. "The invoice slips from Joe at Libations Bar and Grill, coming from the same distributor you use, showed what I've been missing from our invoices: the quantity per box. Now obviously, their pricing can be different, depending on the deal. For instance, a box of Patron normally comes in a box of four, but you're being charged for a box of ten if I'm doing an average wholesale price per bottle."

"What the hell are you saying, Daniella?"

I took a deep breath. "I'm saying I think Heather is stealing from you. And she has someone in the distributor's office or on the delivery truck helping her."

His expression turned angry. "You can't be serious. What proof do you have?"

"I have enough that you should want to look at the inventory on Thursday to see for yourself. If you don't want me here, fine. It's not like I'm trying to overstay my welcome, just attempting to do my job."

"Which includes accusing a long-time employee of theft. One who you profess not to care for and have had issues with."

I stood up, my temper snapping. "You hired me to find out why your numbers weren't adding up."

"Clearly, you're looking in the wrong place."

"You've had a loss every month for the last two years. At first it was hundreds, easily written off. But now it appears to be at least twenty thousand a week. You want to know why you're numbers aren't making sense and why it'll trigger an audit for the IRS. It's because you're losing inventory."

Since Shane looked so pissed off, my eyes shifted towards Max. He was running a hand through his hair but had stood quiet. Gathering my documents that showed the trend, I handed them to him. "You're welcome to look for yourself. And don't worry. My last day will be today."

"Fuck," Max cursed, looking over my notes.

"You don't actually believe her, do you?" Shane asked.

Forget fighting the hurt. I was hurt. And pissed. I knew the man had trust issues, but the fact he'd put me in that camp stung. "Believe whatever the fuck you want to. I'll be in touch next month with your tax return, but I won't need to be on site for it."

I intended to gather my shit and leave, but Max's voice stopped me cold.

"Six months ago, I was here for stocking. I noticed a a missing box of champagn and questioned Heather."

Shane's furious gaze settled on his friend. "What did she say?"

"She said she had partied and admitted to taking it home."

"What the hell, man? And you didn't tell me."

"She made me promise not to, afraid you'd be furious. She gave me five hundred dollars later that day, saying she'd always intended to pay it back. I believed her. She's been here the entire time we have and has always been a loyal, trusted employee. It would be no different than if you'd done the same."

"Fuck. I'm going over to see her at her place. She'll tell me the truth."

"Do you want me to come with?"

Shane shook his head. "No."

Without so much as a backward glance, he strode out, evidently on his way to wake Heather up.

I stood there in shock until Max's voice broke through. "He's running on adrenaline, honey. Try not to take it personally."

I gave a humorless laugh. "Yeah, like he didn't accuse me of making it personal with Heather. Anyways..." I made myself smile and not get emotional. Never could I have imagined things ending this way. But maybe it was for the best. Maybe leaving Shane and this club should be easy because I was pissed instead of sad. "It was a pleasure, Max."

"I'm sorry it had to end the way it did. What are your plans?"

"A nice nap and a flight leaving tomorrow afternoon."

He looked surprised. "New client?"

I shook my head. "Long overdue vacation." I'd requested the time off last week, using the excuse I'd had to work during the holidays.

"Some place warm, I hope."

I smiled. "Jamaica, at an all-inclusive resort where all I want to do is lie in the sun, read a book, and eat good food."

"Sounds amazing. And if there is anything you need: a recommendation, help with your move—"

I'd enjoyed the rush of forensic accounting and had started to think I might have found my niche. It certainly beat the hell out of boring taxes. And if other clubs could trust my discretion, then I might be able to quickly build a client base. "I may take you up on that recommendation for other clubs such as this."

"New client for your firm?"

"Actually, I've been thinking about doing some freelancing. Maybe I have a thing for sex clubs now."

He chuckled. "Please, please make sure you run them past me. Not all of them are reputable."

"Deal. Take care, Max." I gave him a hug, gathered my computer bag, and took one last look before leaving.

Chapter Twenty-Two

SHANE

*I*t took exactly five minutes for Heather to break down and give up the name of her partner in crime. What I hadn't expected, and should have, was that Eric, Daniella's ex, had also been involved. He'd helped hide the money over the last couple of years for a cut. Sure, that fucker hadn't technically stolen from me, but he'd helped cover up for someone who was and had made a tidy profit from it.

The worst part was Heather's reasoning. It wasn't for a sick family member or because she owed money to someone. Nope, it was because she wanted to live in Tribeca and needed the money so she could pay for her condo. One, I might add, that was nicer than my own. Simply put, she somehow had convinced herself she was owed a lifestyle she couldn't afford.

I couldn't believe that after confessing, she even had the audacity to ask to keep her job. Not only was she fired, but she was also lucky we weren't pressing charges. Of course, I needed to discuss it with Max, but the last thing we needed was either the scrutiny or embarrassment. As it was, it would be hard to explain the situation to the other employees. And after I made a call to the distributer later, Heather wouldn't be the only one out of a job. As for Eric, I hadn't decided what his fate would be, but I planned to give him a call to ensure he returned Daniella's money by the end of the week. Otherwise, his big secret would be public in a hurry.

Daniella. Fuck. I'd hurt her. In my defense, I'd been operating on no sleep, and her bombshell had caught me completely off guard.

I walked up the steps to my office slowly and deliberately. There I met the eyes of Max, who was anxiously waiting.

Based on my grim expression, he knew instantly how it had turned out.

"Did she at least give a reason?"

I poured a whiskey and sighed. "Her condo overlooking the city. Her plastic surgery. A lifestyle she feels entitled to."

"I was really hoping for a better excuse, like a sick relative."

"Me, too. She gave up the name of the distributer."

"Fucker. I take it you'll call the supplier and get him fired tomorrow?"

"Chances are she's already called him, and he's taken off. And for a cut, Eric helped shift around money to hide it from being obvious."

He cursed again. "Will you have the pics go viral?"

"I haven't decided. Heather actually had the nerve to ask if she could remain working here."

"She's lucky we won't press charges. We aren't, right?"

I shook my head. "Not worth it. Where's Daniella?"

He leveled me with a look. "Dude. Where do you think she is? She took off after you basically accused her of being jealous of Heather. I believe you also implied that her wanting to stay another morning to give you proof was because she wasn't ready to let you go."

"I didn't mean—shit."

He held up a hand. "If that's your excuse, then it's probably best you don't see her again."

"I don't want that. Is she back at the hotel?"

He shrugged. "Not sure, but I do know she's not coming back here. Matter of fact, she has a flight out tomorrow, leaving on vacation."

This was news. Although come tomorrow, was it really my business? I didn't like the answer.

"I fucked up." I had. Although I hadn't known Daniella that long, I should've handled what she was saying better and not made it personal.

"Guess you could start with that."

Here's hoping it would work.

———

DANIELLA

Even after packing everything up and taking a shower, I was restless. I told myself I didn't care that he hadn't knocked. But it was a lie. I cared. Too much.

As evidence, I realized I'd wanted too badly to prove myself in his eyes. Earn his impossible trust by finding the damn boxes in the frigid cold and figuring out the mystery of his lost revenue. But my quest had left me cold, both literally and figuratively. I wasn't any closer to earning his trust. And I was a fool for not realizing my motivation ran deeper than simply doing my job and an even bigger one for allowing myself to be hurt by it.

That alone made me glad I was leaving tomorrow. I needed to get Shane out of my system.

The knock at the door instantly caused butterflies. I opened it to the object of my thoughts.

He stepped inside, cupping my face. "I'm sorry. So sorry for doubting you. My only defense is I was exhausted, and I didn't want to believe someone who has been with Max and me from the beginning could do such a thing. I fucked up, Dani."

I swallowed hard. "You hurt me by assuming I'd made it personal towards her."

"I know. And I'm sorry. You were right. She'd been stealing with the help of the distributor who kept the box counts off the receipts. And Eric had been helping her to hide the numbers, making it harder for me to see it."

Of all the things he could've said, Eric's involvement shouldn't have shocked me, but it did. "I'm sorry."

He shook his head. "For what? If it wasn't for you, who knows if we ever would've found out the truth? I not only owe you an apology, but a big thank you, too."

Before I could respond, his lips descended to mine, the kiss so unexpected that I pulled back in shock, meeting his eyes.

"I've never wanted this more than I do right now."

A mix of vulnerability and sincerity were reflected in his gaze. If this was our last night, who was I to deny something I'd longed for every time we were together? I didn't hesitate to pull his mouth back to mine, aware he was moving me into the room and letting the door shut behind him.

His tongue tangled with mine, making me desperate for this intimate contact to continue. One taste wasn't enough. Instead, it felt like I'd been starved for it and was finally getting my fix. He must've felt the same as he didn't break contact, instead deepening the kiss and throwing everything in his arsenal at it with lips, tongue, and teeth. His hand tangled in my hair while the other went straight for my pussy.

"So fucking perfect every time," he whispered, moving his kisses to my ear and throat. "I want nothing between us."

"God. Yes." Meanwhile, the logical part of my brain thought, why? Why on the last day? But it was overruled by lust. Yep, now I knew how after-school specials were made.

And I couldn't even say my intentions were good. Because they were, oh, so dirty instead. Which is why, when he buried himself deep inside of me, skin on skin, coming deep inside of me, I reveled in our last time together.

After falling asleep in his arms, I awoke with a start the next morning. Checking my phone, I breathed a sigh of relief at the time reflected. I had a plane to catch in four hours. Glancing over, I saw Shane still fast asleep. Considering he'd pulled an all-nighter and then had marathon sex with me, I couldn't say I was surprised.

Even after I'd showered and dressed, he was still passed out. I was tempted to wake him, but for what? A sad good-bye? A stupid hope that he'd want me to stay? I thought about a note, but the same problem persisted. What would I say? It was fun?

Turns out it had been a hell of a lot more than that.

Chapter Twenty-Three

SHANE

I woke up slowly, taking a moment to remember where in the hell I was. Then I smiled and reached for Daniella, only to find her side of the bed empty. And cold. I sat up, rubbing the sleep from my eyes. Jesus, I'd slept like the dead.

I listened for the shower but didn't hear it. Then I realized the suitcase I'd noticed by the door last night was gone. And so was everything Daniella.

Ten minutes later, Max looked up from his desk to see me walking towards him with purpose.

"Where is Dani? Did she come by here?"

He shook his head. "No, man. Weren't you with her? When you didn't come back yesterday, I assumed you two made up."

"We did, but she left."

He checked his watch. "Probably for her flight."

Shit. I'd forgotten about the trip. "Where was she going?"

"Jamaica, mon."

I didn't even crack a smile. Instead, I ran a hand through my hair in frustration.

"Question to ask is if you're going after her?"

"To what end?"

He leveled me a look. "That's the question you need to ask yourself. But if you want my opinion, I've never seen you happier than you've been the last week with her around."

"I'd be selfish to keep her in this world."

He chuckled. "Considering she's looking at offers to free-lance at other clubs, I'd say she's not in a hurry to leave it."

"The hell she is."

He stood up. "Seems to me if you want a right to weigh in on her decision, you'd better get your ass to JFK."

"And say what? That we've known each a little over a week and I might have feelings?" At this point, old insecurities surfaced, stemming from my mother's decision to disown me. How could a woman like Daniella want to tie herself to man like me? Sure, I had money. But what else could I offer her? Long work hours which included weekends and nights. A parade of women I'd been with in front of others at the club. A tendency to be a dick and to have a tough time apologizing. And what would her family and friends think if they learned the truth about me?

Max sighed. "What if I came to you and said I'd met someone who I wanted to have a relationship with? Would you tell me I wasn't worthy of it because I owned this club? Would you tell me I didn't deserve to be happy with someone I could fall in love with?"

"Of course not."

"Then stop questioning whether or not you deserve it and simply ask her. She's a big girl who can make her own decisions. Not as though she isn't aware you can be a moody son-of-a-bitch. Yet she continues to like you."

I cracked a smile and blew out a breath. "I'm not sure I can do this."

"You act like you need to choose between this club and her. But what if you can have both? Wouldn't that be worth it? I know for me it would be."

My decision came easily. "Can you manage a few days without me?"

DANIELLA

I arrived at the airport exactly one hour after leaving Shane in bed. My first thought while putting my heavy suitcase up on the scale with my muscles screaming from the effort was that I needed a massage. It would be my first order of business once I arrived at the resort. I had every intention of taking a relaxing vacation before returning and figuring out where I'd live and if I wanted to stay in my job. I wasn't sure what I was going to do, but for the first time, I did feel the freedom to choose.

Smiling at the desk agent, I handed her my passport.

"Ms. Trivioli, good news for you today. You've been upgraded to first class."

"Oh. Why?" I didn't mean to sound ungrateful, but it didn't make sense.

She shrugged. "Don't know. Could be a full flight, and your airfare made you eligible. Did you not want it?"

"No, no, I do. Thanks." Considering Eric had sent confirmation about ten minutes ago that he'd wire the rest of my money by the end of the week, perhaps everything was looking up.

After security, I made my way to the lounge where I had a cocktail—okay, maybe three—and tried not to think about Shane. How was it this last week with him was leaving me more broken-hearted than my two years with Eric? I couldn't be in love with him already, could I? Perhaps it was simply lust. I didn't want to think about it. Instead, I got up, ready for my flight and an escape via first class.

I took the window seat in the third row. The setup was awesome with the flat screen in front of me and the additional leg room. I didn't fly much, but this was the way to do it. I couldn't wait to recline and maybe get some much-needed sleep; last night hadn't afforded me much. While the plane filled up, I flipped around the movie channels and figured I might end up with an empty seat beside me. Then he sat down.

Despite tired eyes, a dark scruff, and wearing his clothes from last night, Shane still looked devastatingly handsome.

"What are you doing here?" I posed the obvious question.

He put a small bag under the seat before turning to me. "Heading to Jamaica."

"But why? Wait. Were you the one who upgraded me?"

"Max technically did, but I asked if he could do me the favor while I was busy getting to the airport. I was happy to find out this flight wasn't completely full, and we could get seats together. I don't fly much, so the extra room is nice."

"Uh. Okay, but why are you here?"

For the first time in this little exchange, he appeared nervous.

"When I woke up, you were gone. I realized it's because I didn't give you any indication or reason to stay and—"

He was interrupted by the flight attendant asking us for our drink orders.

"To be continued once we get in the air."

I gripped his arm, impatient for his words. "What? No, say what you were going to."

But it was too late. The announcement were being made, the flight attendant was back to get our cups, and then came the safety briefing. Finally, after what seemed to take forever, we were airborne.

He quickly reclined both his seat and mine fully and then put up the privacy screen. Once we were both reclined flat, we turned towards one another, our heads propped on our hands, eye to eye.

"Hi."

I laughed at his greeting. "Hi."

"Where was I?"

"I believe you were about to answer why you're on a flight to Jamaica with me."

"Right." He exhaled a breath. "I don't want what we have to stop."

His words caused a shiver to run up my body. I was about to respond, but he wasn't done.

"I realize it's crazy to feel this way after a few days. I mean we hardly know one another. You just got out of an engagement, and I've never been in a real relationship. Tell me it's crazy."

I smiled. "It is crazy, but I'd be lying if I said I didn't feel the same way."

He scooted closer to me, pulling my hips in line with his. "I'm an owner of a sex club, and I won't give that up. I can't change my past, and I won't apologize for it. My own mother died still disowning me for my choices."

I reached out, stroking his face where pain was etched in his expression. I fought my own emotion in watching a man like him say such difficult things. "No one should have to feel judged like that."

He swallowed hard. "No, they shouldn't. But being involved with me will mean people in your life will judge. I guess what I'm saying is I don't know what to offer you, Daniella. What I can give to a relationship."

"The same could be said for me. What am I offering you? Monogamous sex that doesn't include your show room at the club and the complications of having a girlfriend."

"You sell yourself short."

"Right back at you. Now, as for what you give me. You give me honesty. Freedom to be myself." I hesitated before blurting it out. "But I've wondered if you miss the club and performing or being with other women. I know we've watched some shows together, and I enjoy it. But I wonder if you prefer to be down there. I even thought about how I'd feel performing with you. I mean I wouldn't want more than just me and you in a scene, but—"

He was already shaking his head. "Baby, there is no way I'm allowing one other person to see you naked. Your body and your orgasms are for me only. I recognize that makes me a hypocrite considering most of the club has seen me, but there's no way I want any other man watching you. And as for the other. You make me feel things I never thought I would. And I've never felt half as attracted to a woman as I am to you."

I smiled at his admission.

"Did you mean it when you said you didn't want to have kids? Because that's not something I can change either. Even if I wanted to."

"I've never wanted them. Frankly, it'll be nice to date someone I don't have to worry about pressuring me later."

He looked relieved. "I can't promise you that by the end of the month you won't be thoroughly sick of me working so many hours or being grumpy or having to apologize for getting this relationship stuff wrong. But it won't fall apart because I'd ever cheat. That I can promise. I trust you, Dani. The bottom line is I can't think of anyone I'd rather try this with than you."

"Me, neither." I appreciated that we were being logical about this. We weren't calling it insta-love or ignoring the fact we each still had a lot to learn about the another. "Would this relationship include kissing?"

He grinned in return. "So much you'll be wishing for the days I didn't."

I shook my head. "Not possible." And because I could, I leaned in and kissed him. The free license to do so had me anxious to get closer to him.

He pulled back to chuckle. "Easy, or they'll know exactly what's going on in seats three A and B."

"Mm. Don't tell me you're shy about the mile-high club?"

He arched a brow. "Are you already a card holder?"

I shook my head. "Nope. Would be my first."

He went to work unzipping my jeans. "Mine, too. Now kiss me before everyone hears your orgasm on this plane."

I didn't have time to relish being his first at something before he had me climaxing around his fingers while he swallowed down my moan. When I opened up my eyes, I watched him taste his fingers with hooded eyes.

"Unbelievable every time."

Reaching for him, I was surprised when he took my hand in his and kissed my wrist softly. "Not so fast. Next time I come, it'll be inside of you, so I can watch it drip down your inner thighs and think about how it's still inside of you when we go to dinner tonight."

"Jesus," I muttered, his dirty words doing nothing to quell my hunger for him. "Guess I know how we'll be spending a good portion of our vacation."

"Daniella Trivioli. Will you do me the honor of trying a real relationship with me?"

I grinned at his proposal. "A hundred times yes."

EPILOGUE

SHANE

*A*fter a busy Friday night at my club, I slipped into bed a happy man. Because Daniella was already sound asleep in it.

Four months after I'd first set eyes on her, I was still just as convinced I'd never get enough. Although I still enjoyed owning and operating the club, I didn't feel truly at peace until I held her in my arms. Which wasn't happening nearly enough for my liking. Sure, we spent at least three nights together per week. But with her condo sublet near her office in Jersey City while I maintained my loft in Manhattan close to the club, that wasn't nearly enough.

When my arms went around her, she sighed in contentment, snuggling closer.

"Mm, how was your night?"

"Better now." I kissed the side of her neck, feeling emotion over this woman who made me laugh, challenged me, but best of all, made me unbelievably happy.

"Me, too."

She was gloriously naked, with her smooth skin rubbing against mine. Although I enjoyed stripping her out of her clothing, especially when she'd come from work to the club in her pencil skirts and fuck-me heels, I loved the best this skin-on-skin connection with her in my bed in the wee hours of the morning.

After reaching around, I groaned when I found her wet and ready for me. I wasted no time pushing inside of her, gripping her hip and rubbing her centerpoint of pleasure until she was wildly bucking against me, begging me to thrust. But I waited until she was teetering on the edge before I set a rhythm, taking her over and up again to an orgasm that squeezed my cock like a vice grip.

But I wasn't done. I pulled out and put her on her back before thrusting deep inside of her again, putting my fore-arms next to her head and diving into her kiss. I'd often scoffed at the word intimacy, but now I knew the true meaning of it.

That's why after I'd made love to her with a second round, I lay with her entwined with my body, not wanting to sever the connection.

"Move in with me," I said in the dark, hoping she wasn't already asleep.

She popped up and looked down on me, moonlight making her look even more beautiful. "What did you say?"

"Move in with me. Or if you don't like my place, then we can find another one together. Especially after you start your new job." She'd given notice after tax time, intending to start free-lancing in the city, doing everything from accounting to fraud investigations. Clearly, she already had one loyal client in the club. She'd also earned Joe's business at the sport's bar around the corner.

"Your loft is amazing, but, uh, how did this come up tonight?"

"I've been thinking about it for a while now. Matter of

fact, the guys at work mentioned I'm a real dick Monday through Thursday unless I've spent the night with you."

"So, I should move in with you because Max and your employees would appreciate it?"

Her voice was quiet and I knew immediately I'd screwed this up. Time to lay it out. "No, you should do it because I love you and don't want to spend our nights apart anymore."

She blew out a breath. "You love me?"

I started to feel a kernel of fear that she might not feel the same. "I really screwed up the order of things. Probably should've told you that part before asking you to move in or making it seem like it had been the idea of the guys at work."

I flipped her on her back so I could be eye to eye with her. "Let me start over. I love you, Daniella. More than I ever thought possible to love someone. And when I'm with you, I'm happy. When I know you're in my bed at home waiting for me, I'm anxious to get here. I wasn't sure how I'd adapt to a relationship, but the last four months have taught me the reason I didn't want one before now was because I didn't have you."

"Wow. When you do a do-over, you reach for the stars. That was—Well, it was everything. I love you, too. So much."

I hadn't realized how much I needed to hear those words until they came from her lips.

"Guess that means we're out of the trying phase?" she quipped.

"Must mean we're in a full-blown relationship now."

"Does that freak you out?"

I shook my head. "Not at all. Actually, I don't think we're done trying, after all."

"Why is that?"

I tucked her hair behind her ear, nuzzling her neck. "Because I have every intention of trying to make you happy every day."

She smiled. "I have the same intentions."

"Good. Now let's ensure at least half of them are dirty."

ABOUT AUBREY BONDURANT

Aubrey Bondurant is a working mom who loves to write, read, and travel.

She describes her writing style as: "Adult Contemporary Erotic Romantic Comedy," which is just another way of saying she likes her characters funny, her bedroom scenes hot, and her romances with a happy ending.

When Aubrey isn't working her day job or spending time with her family, she's on her laptop typing away on her next story. She only wishes there were more hours of the day!

She's a former member of the US Marine Corps and passionate about veteran charities and giving back to the community. She loves a big drooly dog, a fantastic margarita, and football.

Sign up for Aubrey's newsletter here

Stalk her here:

Website

Facebook

Twitter

Email her at aubreybondurant@gmail.com

OTHER BOOKS BY AUBREY BONDURANT:

Something Series:

Made in the USA
Monee, IL
16 January 2020